Promise Me
Forever

Promise Me Forever

Colette Collins

HARVEST HOUSE PUBLISHERS
Eugene, Oregon 97402

Other Rhapsody Romance Books:

Another Love	*Joan Winmill Brown*
The Candy Shoppe	*Dorothy Leigh Abel*
The Heart That Lingers	*June Masters Bacher*
If Love Be Ours	*Joan Winmill Brown*
Love's Tender Voyage	*Joan Winmill Brown*
One True Love	*Arlene Cook*
Reflection of Love	*Susan C. Feldhake*
Until Then	*Dorothy Leigh Abel*
Until There Was You	*June Masters Bacher*
The Whisper of Love	*Dorothy Leigh Abel*
With All My Heart	*June Masters Bacher*

PROMISE ME FOREVER

Copyright © 1983 by Harvest House Publishers
Eugene, Oregon 97402

Second printing, March 1984
ISBN 0-89081-397-3

Printed in the United States of America.

Chapter 1

*T*he silver wings of the 747 dropped below the clouds and April Anderson surveyed the broad expanse of the calm waters of the Pacific Ocean. The pilot's resounding voice said, "Ladies and gentlemen, those of you on the right side of the aircraft can get a magnificient view of Diamond Head."

April's pulse quickened as she glimpsed the spectacular view of the famous volcano which had become a landmark on the island of Oahu. She was glad she had requested a window seat when she boarded the plane in Minneapolis. The sight of the tropical paradise from her lofty view left her almost breathless.

A stewardess swept through the cabin checking to see that all seats were in their upright position while another announced over the public address system, "We are now approaching Honolulu International Airport. Please observe the no smoking signs and fasten your seat belts for landing." Methodically seat belts snapped into place.

April tucked her novel into her carry-on bag which had been stowed beneath the seat in front of her. Her reading material the last several hours left her yearning for a twist of fate that would steer Mr. Heartthrob into her life.

"No use dreaming fairytales," April tried to convince herself. "With my luck, Prince Charming will come charging in on a Honda and want help with the payments." She grinned as she visualized the scene.

As the plane continued to descend, April reached into her handbag searching for her Pink Geranium lip gloss and hand mirror. She mechanically applied it to her paled lips and then reached for her hairbrush to give her short bouncy blonde hair a fluffing. She checked to see if the blusher applied hours earlier across her high cheek bones was still sporting a rosy glow. Her light blue eyeshadow accented her warm azure eyes. Satisfied with her appearance, she placed her makeup bag back into her purse and then smoothed the creases from her raw silk pant suit. She silently thanked her co-worker Kristen for talking her into splurging on this purchase for the trip. The light-weight jacket covered her royal blue camisole. The combination was perfect as she left behind the chilling March winds and prepared to step into the balmy temperature of Hawaii.

The pilot made his final approach and with the greatest of ease set the huge aircraft with its tons of passengers and their luggage down with hardly a bump. Yet all the butterflies in April's stomach seemed to be let loose as the plane slowly came to a stop. "There's no turning back now," she summarized as she gathered together her personal carry-on baggage.

As excited as she was about being in Honolulu for the first time, April was apprehensive of her assignment of managing her uncle's art gallery and setting up a pre-opening benefit for T.J. Richard's art exhibition. Uncle David had recently purchased the Gottery Gallery but with the economic situation, the manager, Mr. Chow, wasn't able to cope with the stress and unexpectedly walked out. Not only had business been slow, but just last month the rent on the ground-floor space in the huge office complex had doubled.

A graduate of Minnesota Design School, April

had gained two years' experience as an art dealer in her uncle's gallery in Minneapolis. Yet she wasn't prepared for the surprise she got when Uncle David called her into his office and asked her to accept the challenge of the newest acquisition. He had said, "Not everyone has a sixth sense of what's going on in the art world, but you know how to pick a mood and are daring enough to go with your sensibilities."

April inwardly wished she had as much confidence in herself. She was quite sure she could handle the routine affairs of the gallery but she had never organized a pre-opening benefit alone. T.J. was one of her uncle's favorite new artists who had a flare for an international movement called "new wave," or "new image." His canvases showed an explosive splatter of lavender and purple hues blending delicately into blues. His work was selling well and it seemed the type of art that would appeal to the islanders. April also admired his work but she was intimidated by his strong ego. If the benefit wasn't a success, T.J. would blame it on her and not his work.

"You can do it. You can do it," mumbled April to restore her slipping confidence. However, bent on pushing work out of her mind until Monday morning rolled around, April reset her watch for the time change. She had the whole evening and all day Sunday for sightseeing and sun. The travel brochures she had picked up at the agency depicted sunny enchanted islands with a variety of things to do and see. They boasted of "gleaming white beaches, exotic shops, restaurants of many cultures and…best of all, happy, friendly people who make your stay truly unforgettable."

Wishing she could have brought Kristen along to share this experience, April began deplaning with the other passengers. Her carry-on bag was draped from her left shoulder and she carried her briefcase in her left hand and her purse tucked under her right arm.

The arriving passengers, anticipating being met by friends or relatives, streamed into the terminal searching the mass of faces for a familiar sight. April watched as the island visitors were met and colorful flower leis were slipped over their heads. In typical "aloha" spirit, a customary kiss was placed on the cheek. Even the large tourist groups were met by guides in gaudy orange-print shirts and white slacks and girls in strapless sundresses. The true Hawaiians' dark skin and hair contrasted sharply to the arriving pale passengers. They mechanically placed baby orchid leis around the tourists' necks and then posed with each person for a color picture of his arrival in the Hawaiian islands.

A twinge of envy rushed through April as she watched the beautiful procedure of giving and receiving the purple and white orchid leis. The fragrance in the air was divine. There was no one to meet her and she felt a sweep of loneliness. But before the Swedish lass could become absorbed in self-pity, she held her head high and reminded herself she was just plain lucky to be here. Tall and svelt with a tiny waist, April looked around the terminal for signs which would point her in the direction of the baggage area.

At the revolving baggage counter, the Louis Vitton bags contrasted sharply with the brown cardboard boxes tied loosely with string, creating a haphazard circle of luggage. April spotted her ordinary canvas bag and pointed it out to the porter waiting patiently by her side. Stepping back she watched his muscular arms effortlessly lift the heavy bag onto his hand truck. As they made their way through the throngs of people, April felt the high humidity and noticed the perspiration dripping from his dark rugged face. But his friendly smile assured April she could count on him to see her and her bags safely into a cab.

April's eyes were wide, bright and animated as she stepped into the tropical warmth. "Wait until I send those postcards to the staff back home," she mused to herself. "Won't they be envious." Only two days into spring and Mother Nature had dealt a cruel blow by dumping five inches of snow on the almost barren ground in her hometown.

She squinted in the bright sunlight as she fished into her handbag for her sunglasses. Though she conveyed girl-next-door ordinariness, at the same time her tall frame had that glamorous presence that demanded attention as she and the porter waited for a taxi.

He whistled and soon a blue and white taxi appeared from seemingly nowhere and stopped in front of her. The driver stepped out and opened the trunk for her luggage as the porter politely opened the car door.

"Hey, George, where are all the cabs?" April looked up startled to see who had spoken in the slight southern accent. From her position in the backseat, she looked up into a bronzed face with the growth of today's beard and a pair of the most remarkable brown eyes she had ever seen. It wasn't a question of the density of the brown, but it was a combination of things: warmth, humor, interest and a curious kind of mocking sadness. In her momentary glance she saw the man to be tall, slender, athletic-looking, and probably in his early thirties. The breeze caught his black hair and it tumbled across his forehead. April began staring at him intently, then looked around guiltily wondering if anyone had noticed. The stranger wore a beige summer suit and his dark brown shirt matched his eyes. He carried a leather attache case and his appearance gave every indication he was a young executive arriving home from a business trip.

"Welcome home," the porter greeted him as a broad smile spread across his face in response to seeing a familiar traveler, and then continued, "Sorry, there ain't enough cabs tonight. One of the tour buses broke down and all the cabs are doing a whopping business taking tourists to Waikiki."

"Nothing has gone right for me today," lamented the weary man. "I had a six-hour delay in leaving Sydney and then we were forced to land in Tahiti. It's been a long day," he sighed as his hand brushed his hair out of his face.

As he spoke, April again peered out the open door and realized the look of sadness she saw in his eyes was probably just tiredness.

"This beautiful young lady is headed to Waikiki. I'll bet she wouldn't mind sharing her cab with you," the jolly porter said to the weary globetrotter. April saw him wink devilishly at the driver.

Before she could answer, the self-assured man threw his hanging bag into the front seat and manuevered his long legs into the back next to April. She felt her cheeks flush as she weakly answered, "Of course not," to the stranger.

As the driver banged his door closed and turned on the ignition, April peeked out of the corner of her eye to get a better look at the man next to her. Even though he was obviously exhausted, he had the look of a man who knew who he was and where he was going.

"Say, thanks a lot," he replied. "It's been such a frustrating day and I'm anxious to get home." There was something magnetic about the man and so disarming about his smile.

Unprepared for the way the chemistry started bubbling in her veins, April giddily said, "With an accent like yours, you must live on the south side of Waikiki." The slight twang in his voice was distinctively different from her midwest crispness.

He ignored her attempt at humor and seemed strangely elusive as he dryly said, "I'm originally from Kentucky." His eyes searched her form and finally came to rest on her hands nervously playing with her handbag. "By the way, my name is Derick," and he tilted his head to look squarely into her eyes.

"I'm April," came the reticent response as she let her eyes meet his for a fleeting moment and then focused on the passing scenery.

"April? That's an easy one to remember. 'A-pr-il L-o-ve,' " he began to sing in an off-key version of Pat Boone's rendition of the 50s hit. It seemed he wanted to dish out the teasing and not be the brunt of it.

Flashing an embarrassed grin, she began to explain. "What can I say? It was Mom and Dad's favorite tune so I didn't have a chance when I arrived in the merry month of April showers."

"Is this your first time in Hawaii?" he inquired.

"Yes," she replied delighted he was seemingly taking an interest in her. "I'm from Minnesota."

"Minnesota," he sneered. "Why would anybody want to live in that vast frozen land?"

"Well, I, um..." April stuttered trying to think of a quick retort. Irritated that he was belittling her home state she snapped, "Minnesota happens to be a great place to live. Have you ever been there?"

"Just made a quick trip through there one January. The 20-degrees-below-zero weather didn't agree with my warm blood," he said trying to ease himself out of the unfriendly situation he had put himself in.

April smiled at a private thought of him trying to keep warm in his lightweight suit.

"Do you still have family in Kentucky?" April quizzed him.

"Yes," he replied and offered no more information, making April feel like she was prying into his personal affairs.

The cab driver, not paying any attention to the stiff attempt at conversation in the backseat, steered his taxi onto Nimitz Highway leading into the city of Honolulu.

"I suppose you're here to turn your white parchment skin to a golden bronze," he said as he folded his arms and looked intently at her porcelain-like face. "Just be careful you don't burn your pretty little bod."

April, taken back by his comment which was almost a compliment, retorted, "I don't know if I'll have time but I do hope I can get a little tan while I'm here."

"Not surprising," he said with a teasing glint in his eye. "An attractive blonde alone in the Hawaiian Islands. I imagine you will be kept quite busy." His tone hinted on sarcasm.

"For your information," she said with her voice sounding brittle, "I'm not here on vacation." This man next to her could be so kind and caring one minute and the next she found herself bristling at his insinuations. As she talked she unconsciously rubbed her hand across the brown vinyl upholstery car seat that separated her from Derick.

"Oh?" he questioned as he lifted his bushy eyebrows and let his gaze run speculatively over April. "Then let me guess. I'll bet you're here to get married to a sailor."

His assumption of why she was alone infuriated her. His needling was getting to her and before he had a chance to ask any more questions she explained in a tone that displayed more confidence than she was actually feeling: "I'm here to work in my uncle's art gallery. He recently acquired it but the manager walked out last week. I'm going to run it until I can find a suitable manager. We're going to have a one-man exhibition in three weeks hoping that will attract more business. With the economic situation at the moment, business hasn't been too good. And to top it off, the owner of the building doubled our rent. Can you imagine that?'' she ranted in her most business-like manner. She felt uncomfortable as his eyes seemed to penetrate through her skin and she saw the smirk on his face as she finished her speech. She figured he was probably thinking that just because she was a blonde she wasn't capable of rational behavior.

Realizing she had given more information than she had intended, April turned to face Derick and confronted him, ''Just what do you do for a living?''

In his confident and cool manner, the simple but direct answer was ''Investments.''

April's face revealed a blank expression and he went on to say, ''The key to success is diversification.'' He deliberately emphasized each word.

The phrase meant nothing to April yet the words were clearly etched in her mind from the way he had spoken them.

''Were you on business in Australia?'' she quietly asked wondering if the question was being too nosy. Derick, unlike any of the men she had known in Minneapolis, intrigued her. Maybe it was only the charm of his southern voice that toyed with her emotions.

"Yes," he answered tartly. "My partner and I are building a condominium complex in Kona. That's on the Big Island," he felt the need to explain to her. "I'm putting together the financial package from foreign investors." As he talked about his work, his voice mellowed and April noticed an enormous amount of energy spilling forth from his words. Even though he still showed signs of weariness, he came alive as he talked about his project.

"We've put up several condo units and a high-rise office building here in Honolulu," he said. "In fact, if you'll look toward those mountains..." He leaned in April's direction, aligning his face next to hers, and proceeded to point out the high-rise building. His left hand gently touched her shoulder and she felt an electric current race to her brain as she inwardly tried to calm herself.

"Oh, that's wonderful," she exclaimed. Proud to be riding with such an important executive, her defenses slipped and she flashed him a genuine warm smile.

As he settled back into his seat, he continued to talk. "We hope to start groundbreaking on our project in Hawaii in less than a month. We will have 75 units and each one will sell for over a million dollars. Two weeks ago I was in Hong Kong and Singapore and with what I was able to accomplish in Australia this trip, we've almost got all the backing we need. I'll find out tonight whether my partner Pat has cleared the deals on the land.''

Not only was April overwhelmed with the ambitions of the young entrepreneur next to her, but she couldn't believe the way he casually spoke about traveling to distant countries. It was the way she talked about going to Minneapolis suburbs.

"Sounds like you do a lot of traveling," April said, flabbergasted. Then hoping her next question wasn't being too personal, she asked, "Don't you miss your family terribly while you're away?"

Curtly he replied, "I'm not into a lifestyle of a wife and kids. My work takes all my time." His tone cut like steel causing April to realize it was a painful subject. She couldn't help but wonder what had happened to make him so bitter about a family.

He offered no further information as April studied the profile of his firm-set jawline with his unshaven face. Then she turned to look out her window, watching the passing palm trees, crowded industrial buildings, and fluffy clouds in the blue sky as the taxi turned onto Ala Moana Boulevard.

After several minutes of strained silence, April dared to ask, "Is it much further to Waikiki?"

"We're almost there," he solemnly replied.

As they neared the city April caught a view of the magnificent sight of the yacht harbor with hundreds of sailboats docked and others slowly sailing by as the orange sun was setting. To her left was a huge shopping complex and she made a mental note to explore it later.

Unpredictable as he was, Derick made another attempt at being polite. He began pointing out a number of Honolulu's finest restaurants which he emphasized April should be sure to try—seafood restaurants with fabulous views, steak houses, and a number of restaurants that served Oriental cuisine. His manner oozed with kindness as he talked.

"Thanks," April timidly responded,, "but I really don't like to go to fancy places alone." The words tumbled out before she realized it probably sounded like an invitation for him to take her out.

"I guarantee," he responded in his southern drawl, "if you go alone, you won't leave alone." Then he grinned as his eyes searched April. Her face flushed.

"I'm afraid that's not my style," she answered softly and looked the other way, wishing her modesty wasn't always so apparent from the color rising in her cheeks.

The taxi come to a stop in front of a high-rise hotel. "This is your hotel, miss," the driver said before stepping out to open the trunk.

Derick opened his door and stretching his long legs, stepped outside and offered a hand for April's exit. Hesitatingly, she looked into his eyes and then placed her hand in his as he helped her from the car.

"Thank you," she graciously said and then reluctant to say good-bye, she added, "I really hope everything goes well for you with your condos. I hope someday I have the opportunity to..." Her voice trailed off as she noticed the driver anxious to be paid so he could get on his way. She opened her purse to find her wallet but Derick gallantly motioned for her to put it away. "This one is on me," he generously offered before getting back into the cab. " Aloha."

April stood dumbfounded watching the cab and its puzzling passenger drive away. He reminded April of a model from a Matchabelli magazine ad who had just come to life and then quickly disappeared. He had exuded the sort of confidence and self-assurance more often found in older men. His suave manner and sense of security somehow sent chills up and down her spine. Yet his aloofness cast him into the category of a cocky, abrasive man filled with machismo. In just their brief encounter, his moods had taken on a bittersweet texture.

But now he was gone. He hadn't even asked her last name. She would probably never see him

again. He had not told her what company he was
with. Disappointment showed in April's face as
she registered at the front desk.

"I do hope you'll be happy here and enjoy your
stay in Hawaii," the desk clerk told her.

"Oh, I'm sure I will," April said bringing herself back to reality.

She was handed a key to room #1703 which
would be her home until decisions were made at
the gallery as to how long she would need to stay.

Inside her room, April walked across the sea-
green carpet to the windows and pulled open the
heavy draperies. She gasped as she saw the breathtaking panoramic view of the Pacific Ocean, Diamond Head and a string of hotels along the coast.

The sun had nearly set and April could see people in the distance gathering their personal belongings into beach bags, folding up their towels, and
lazily leaving the beach. The breeze gently blew
through the fronds on the palm trees. What could
be more perfect than spending a month in paradise?
Then as if answering her own question, she realized that the only thing that could make it better
would be having someone with whom she could
share long walks on the beach as the sun was setting. In her mind she pictured them hand in hand,
carrying their shoes, talking, laughing, stopping
at a sidewalk cafe to sip a cool drink.

April walked around the room examining the

kingsize bed with its splashy green, yellow, and white bedspread. The colors were carried out in the wallpaper. A small round glass table with two white wicker chairs faced the window. A dresser with four drawers and a nightstand with the telephone completed the sparse furniture in the room.

April began to unpack the few summer clothes she had brought with her. She put last season's beach wear into a drawer and hung up her sundresses and several skirts and blouses which would be appropriate for work. She lined up her toiletries on the white marble countertop in the bathroom. The yellow and green towels added the only color to the room.

Realizing she was hungry, April dabbed some Charlie perfume behind her ears, donned her white slacks and red-and-blue-striped blouse and left her room in search of a coffee shop.

"A table for one," she said self-consciously to the host who in turn escorted her to a corner table, Fresh red carnations adorned the table and the red linen table cloth sharply contrasted the white china. Upon the recommendation of the waiter, April ordered the mahi mahi, a local fish. As she waited for the main course, she nibbled on her fresh fruit salad of pineapple and papaya. From her seat she could watch couples strolling the beach under the twinkling stars while the emotions of the day began to cloud her thoughts.

After she finished her meal, the strain of the long day began to take its toll. She returned to her room realizing an early bedtime would allow her an early start at sightseeing on Sunday.

She slipped into her short pink nightgown with the white embroidered flowers and then decided to take one more look out the window. She pulled back the drapes and stared into the night. Honolulu had become a tapestry of colorful lights strung along the ocean. A yawn reminded her of the time. She closed the drapes and pulled back the brightly colored bedspread to crawl between the freshly laundered sheets. It was only minutes before she was in the 'Land of Nod.'

Awakened early by severe jet lag, April's eyes focused on the unfamiliar surroundings. Then she remembered yesterday. Her pulse quickened at the thought of Derick but collecting her wits, she said aloud, "Good-bye, Derick," and blew a kiss to her previous rendezvous.

She stretched as she pulled back the covers, grabbed her robe, and headed for one more look out the window. The splendor of the rising sun from her elevated viewpoint excited her.

"Oh, what a beautiful morning. Oh, what a beautiful day," she sang as she danced around her room. "I've got a beautiful feeling, everything's going my way." She twirled around, grabbed her shorts and said, "Look out, world, here I come," as she headed for the bathroom.

She showered and applied the barest of make-up. Along with her T-shirt and shorts, she put on sandals, desiring a walk on the beach before breakfast.

The early morning sun felt good on her bare arms and lean legs. She took off her sandals so that she could walk close to the water's edge. The warmth of the fine white sand felt good as it filtered through her toes. She ventured into the water as she walked letting the warm waves lap around her ankles.

Yesterday Hawaii had been worlds away. To-day tranquil beauty abounded. The endless view of the blue-green expanse contrasted to the mountains in the distance, some of them sharp-edged, some more graceful in form, reaching up to the white cloud formations in the sky.

She looked into the face of every jogger that sprinted past her. Would Derick be among them? Did he exercise regularly to keep in such healthy form? Was this his territory? Her curiosity was strong but she knew finding answers were slim.

Watching people in the early morning hour was fascinating. Older couples, acting like they were on a second honeymoon, strolled along the beach holding hands.

April stopped to watch two young boys, super-vised by their parents sitting a short distance away, building a sand castle. The youngest filled his plastic bucket with water as the older boy haphazardly constructed his concept of a castle. He gently patted the wet sand into place. Then without warning, a wave came further inland taking their castle out to sea.

"That's the way it's got to be with my encounter with Derick," April philosophized to herself. "It was a nice ride together in the cab but now he's gone. Out of my life. I must make new friends." Never before had a man affected her in this way.

April continued to walk and daydream until hunger pangs prompted her to stop for breakfast. She spotted a restaurant where brunch was being served on the patio, so she found a table where she could saturate herself with the ocean view.

Ordering coffee, fresh fruit, bacon and eggs with an English muffin, April began to formulate her plans for the day. She would sunbathe and swim for several hours, then enjoy a catamaran ride to give her a look at the Honolulu shoreline.

When she finished breakfast she walked back to her hotel. She put on her bathing suit and taking her beach towel hurried to the sun. She staked her territory on the white sand as people lazily began arriving at the beach. She was too fascinated watching other tourists to read her novel. She was amused that several young men stopped to talk with her. It was the usual polite questions. "Did you just arrive? Where are you staying? Where are you from?" When she declined their offers to meet later, they quickly moved on.

Knowing her fair skin wouldn't take too much sun the first day here, she went back to her room early to shower and change into shorts. Her hotel was across the street from the International Market Place and she was eager to browse there. She looked at all the display counters, inspecting the wide assortment of rings and necklaces, and browsed through the racks of colorful muumuus and shirts.

The time fled quickly as April fulfilled her day's plans. The exercise combined with the sun seemed to bring tiredness into her body. After an early dinner in the hotel's restaurant, she strolled through the gift shops in the lobby. She selected several postcards and then returned to her room.

She turned on the TV set and began writing her postcards, bragging of the wonderful time she was having. Tonight as she slipped into her bed, her pink skin contrasted greatly with the white sheets. She turned out the lights and quickly drifted off to sleep. Tomorrow could be a hard day, she realized, and she wanted to be ready for it.

Chapter 2

*O*pening her eyes on Monday morning, April stretched, relishing the smoothness of her sheets and the softness of the pillow. Then with a start, she sat upright. Today was her first day on the job. Nervousness began to settle in. What would she find at the gallery? Uncle David had told her they had a young female assistant. Would she resent the owner's niece taking over? What kinds of paintings and sculpture had been acquired but not sold? Would there be any semblence of organization? But the big question tumbled about her mind. Would she, April Anderson, be able to revitalize the gallery out of its financial slump and put it on the road to prosperity?

"Well, there's only one way to find out," April mused to herself as she decided to face the challenge head-on. She sprang into action, throwing back the covers, and grabbed her personal items as she headed for the shower.

"Dear God, please help my sinking confidence," she uttered in the form of a quick prayer.

From her closet, April chose her favorite outfit—a full white skirt with pink and blue flowers and a matching blouse with short puffy sleeves. Her accessories included a wide blue belt and light blue sandals. She added tiny pearl earrings and a white bracelet. She looked at herself in the mirror and the rosy glow from yesterday's sun alluded health. "Hmmm, ready to tackle anything," she tried to convince herself. "Well, maybe I'll be ready after coffee," she said deliberately, delaying going to the gallery.

The coffee and light breakfast gave her the pep she needed. Her stride was brisk and with her head held high, she crossed the lobby with her maroon leather briefcase in hand. When she felt the warmth of the early morning sun, she decided against a cab and reveled in the ten-block walk to the gallery. She had studied her Honolulu map and could easily find the address.

As she approached the high-rise office complex, her heart fluttered at the unknown. The sign,

"Gottery Gallery," was unobstrusive, but written with flare above the door on the ground floor. From her vantage point on the sidewalk, April peered through one of the two large windows and saw the emptiness of the spacious room.

She took a deep breath and opened the door. A bell sounded and she was greeted by a young Oriental girl who flashed a wide smile. She wore a pale yellow dress which accented her brown skin and long dark hair.

"May I help you?" she kindly asked, radiating a warmth which caused April to feel at ease with her.

"I'm April Anderson. My Uncle David owns the gallery."

"It's so good to have you here," the Chinese girl said. "I'm Tessie." With hardly a pause she continued, "Let me show you around." Tessie steered April around the room with its gleaming white tile floor and stark white walls.

Four huge paintings were framed and hung at one end of the room and an abstract bronze sculpture was displayed on a glass pedestal. Several other paintings were propped against the wall. Three large ferns were hung in baskets from the ceiling and were the only signs of life in the otherwise sterile room.

"As you can see, we need more paintings and the bills are mounting up. The owner is threatening to break our lease unless we pay the back rent immediately." Then realizing the responsibility she was placing on the new art dealer, Tessie quickly added, "I think you'll like it here."

"Wow," exclaimed April whirling around to see the studio, "it sounds like there is a lot to be done around here."

"I'll show you your office," Tessie said and led the way to a small inner office. There was a large walnut desk piled high with stacks of paper and books, a beige phone, a calendar that wasn't up-to-date, and a brightly painted sign that read "God Bless This Mess." Amidst the seeming rubble was a shiny silver bowl with a yellow double hibiscus floating in water. A handwritten card stood beside it that simply read, "Welcome."

As she bent down to smell the fragrance, April said, "Thanks, Tessie. This is the first flower I've received in Hawaii. It means a lot to me." A rapport had been established that would make working together easy.

"How about some coffee?" Tessie asked as she picked up the stainless steel coffeepot and began pouring into china cups.

The sound of the doorbell sent Tessie scurrying out front as April seated herself behind the massive desk. She began sorting through the papers, neatly organizing bills in one stack, general correspondence in another, and information regarding artists and forthcoming events in another.

She began leafing through the accounting books and to her horror discovered many overdue bills. She winced when she saw two months of rent was overdue and in just over a week another month would be due. The telephone bill hadn't been paid for months and the electric bill was past due.

Her thoughts were interrupted by the shrill ring of the phone. At least the phone hadn't been cut off. She answered it only to find the voice at the other end complaining because he hadn't received any money for a past bill. She sweetly tried to explain she had only arrived on the job today and was looking into the matter of overdue bills. The administrative work was her least favorite thing about running an art gallery and this one definitely presented some real challenges. She was interrupted again. Tessie wanted her to speak personally to an artist in the gallery.

Back in her little office again, she was disturbed by the ringing telephone again. This time it was a client reneging on a painting he had bought. That money sure would have helped with the bills. "Maybe I'm already in over my head," she cringed, "I can't give up on my first day," and she buried her head in the pile of papers on her desk.

Feeling depressed, she glanced at her watch and realized lunch and a walk outdoors might give her a better perspective on things. On Tessie's recommendation, she found a little cafe only a block away. As she nibbled, she began formulating a plan of action. She would write letters to each company the gallery owed money to asking for an extension of payment. She rationalized that if she were straightforward in explaining the difficulties, they would understand. Maybe if she personally talked to their landlord, a Mr. Donovan, about the rent he would appreciate her honest attempt at dealing with the problem. She would promise to pay the back rent as soon as she could collect on some back invoices.

April felt much better as she hurried back to the office. As she walked she began practicing her speech to Mr. Donovan. She wanted to be business-like in her appearance and not appear to be an inexperienced young girl. She visualized Mr. Donovan in a fashionable decorated office, herself seated in a plush chair across from his desk. He would be in a high leather wing-tipped chair, asking a trim, brunette secretary to hold all his calls while he talked with Miss Anderson. She imagined him as a big burly man, but beneath his gruff exterior would be a teddy-bear quality. Taking a puff on his cigar, he would face April and with a twinkle in his eye, he would say to the young business-woman before him, "Well, since you've only arrived on the job today, we'll be happy to give you an extension. I happen to be an art lover myself."

Back at her office, April tackled the assignment of writing letters explaining her new position with the gallery and reassuring the creditors the gallery would soon be able to pay their bills.

She even made a few phone calls to people owing the gallery, politely saying, "I hate to do this to you, but are you going to be able to pay a little on your painting this month?"

Receiving positive responses, April began to feel her spirits lift. When she could think of no more delay tactics, the time had come for her to face Mr. Donovan directly. Mustering all the courage she could, April rode the elevator in her building to the eleventh floor. Taking a deep breath, she opened the impressive wooden double doors leading to his office and smiled innocently at the receptionist.

"I'd like to see Mr. Donovan." she said hoping her voice wasn't wavering as she made her request.

"Do you have an appointment?" the trim brunette routinely asked. She fit exactly the description April had conjured in her mind.

Loosing a little confidence, April fumbled at her words, "Well, I, uh, no, but it's about the rent."

"Sorry, Mr. Donovan doesn't see anyone without an appointment," which sounded like a much-used line to April. The receptionist turned her back to her typewriter, assuming the matter was closed.

Taken aback by the cool reception, April made one last plea, "I really need to see him today. It's about the past..."

Before the words could come out, the door behind the receptionist opened and a tall figure in tan slacks with a designer knit golf shirt strode briskly into the reception area. April jolted as she saw the familiar face, even though now it was freshly shaven. Her heart skipped a beat and knees turned to jello. He started to speak to his secretary and then he spotted April standing awkwardly beside the desk with her eyes demurely cast down and her mouth opened in shock.

Her mouth felt like it was stuffed with cotton and she could feel the color rising in her cheeks. She had secretly hoped one day she would run into Derick but she never dreamed it would be like this. She was totally caught off guard.

"What are you doing here?" he demanded. His voice was stern, but then with a chuckle he added, "Couldn't get me out of your mind, so you decided to track me down, huh?" His voice was low and there was a sophisticated ease about him.

Furious with his arrogance and being put on the defensive, April icily said, "I'm not here to see you. It's a Mr. Donovan I wish to see." She felt uncomfortable as his eyes scanned her, so she babbled on. "I didn't realize I would need an appointment."

"Come in. Come in," he said as he gently touched her elbow ushering her into his office.

"But, but...I'm, I really don't have time. I needed to see Mr. Donovan just for a few minutes and I really need to get back to work," stammered April, so flustered that she hardly knew whether she should go in or turn and run.

In his soft southern accent, as he graciously opened his office door, he continued, "I'm Derick Donovan." He obviously enjoyed watching her squirm.

"You, you're...Mr. Donovan?" April asked. "You mean you own this building?"

"Yes. Evidently, I'm the ogre that doubled your rent."

She was so speechless as he led her to a chair across from his high polished desk. The scene of his office was the way April visualized it—hunter green carpeting, massive wood bookshelves, decorator sofa with glass coffee table, and the window with the view.

She stared at him in disbelief. Her puzzled look showed in her dazzled eyes. He began apologizing for his dress. "This is typical aloha fashion," he said. "Suits are only for business away from the islands."

"Can I get you something to drink?" he politely

asked his bewildered guest. Seeing her head shake "no" he went on, "Now what was it you wanted to see me about?"

Feeling vulnerable and wishing she could make herself invisible to this character, April began explaining that as soon as she could get the gallery out of its financial slump she would see that the rent was paid first. Disguising her nervousness, she confidently told how she believed the new exhibition would put the gallery back into the black. "Hopefully within three weeks we should be able to pay the rent in full," she told him as she fingered the shoulder strap of her handbag.

After she finished her memorized speech, her eyes had a frozen look.

He sat quietly listening to her. When she finished, he thoughtfully leaned across his desk and said, "I realize you've inherited a bad situation. I'll let you have a three-week extension on the rent."

A weak smile crossed April's face and she relaxed slightly in her chair. But then he went on, "Frankly, my dear girl, I couldn't care less whether you pay on time or not. But if you're going to survive in this business world, you'll have to learn how to make ends meet. For each week that the rent is not paid, I'll add a 7% interest charge. I think this will help you learn the management skills you need."

April's temper flared. "What makes you think you need to teach me business skills?" she demanded. "How dare you think I need your help in running the gallery." She bolted from the chair and blurted "I'll have the money soon to pay you and we'll not be late again, Mr. Donovan!"

"Call me Derick. All my friends do." he continued with a smirk.

Her eyes flashed as she ignored his remark. "I thought you of all people would be a little understanding. I'll pay you just as, just as soon as..." Words failed her as anger took over. She grabbed her purse and blindly stumbled to the door as tears welled up in her eyes. "Sorry for taking your time," she yelled and it was his turn to be speechless.

She rushed past the receptionist and out the heavy doors to the elevators. She punched the down button with all her might and stared at the indicator light until the elevator doors opened on the 11th floor. She was glad she was alone in the elevator. She felt drained and yet rather proud of her feisty spirit. What was it about Derick that caused the blood to rush through her veins? It was his arrogant assumption that infuriated her.

"Of all the nerve, trying to teach me to survive in the business world. I don't need his kind of sympathy. I'll show him. I don't know how, but I'll get that rent money real soon if it's the only thing I successfully do while I am here."

Stubbornness combined with anger blazed in her eyes as she stormed back into the gallery. Before Tessie could even ask how it went, April blurted out, "That horrible, intolerant, inconsiderate, mean man."

"Whew, that bad, huh?" questioned Tessie.

April related the entire story to her assistant who listened with a sympathetic ear.

"Somehow, we've got to get that money," April fussed as she marched back and forth across the white tile floor. "Oh, he makes me so furious!" she exclaimed as she stomped into her little office. There she fiercely sorted through the piles of paper hardly noticing what she was doing. Then as she calmed down she began studying invoices. She placed call after call searching for people who would pay their overdue accounts.

At 6 P.M. when Tessie poked her head into the door to say "good night" time had begun to heal April's wounded feelings.

"Is everything okay?" asked the young assistant. "I was going home, but if there is anything I can do before I leave, I'll stay."

"No, you go ahead," April said glancing at her watch. "I'll just do a little more before I go. Have a nice evening. I'll see you tomorrow."

At last by 7:45 P.M. April was convinced she couldn't do any more that night . She straightened up her desk and shut off the lights.

As she locked the gallery to leave, it was getting dark and a gentle rain was falling. Without an umbrella, she would be drenched if she walked back to her hotel. She walked to the curb to see if any cabs were in the vicinity. The street seemed to be deserted. Deciding to walk to the main thoroughfare, she crossed the street. As she did a car rounded the corner and a torrent of water from its wheels splashed her, leaving her dripping wet.

Frustrated, she stood there in shock wondering what else could go wrong in one day. Knowing how bedraggled she must look, she started to laugh instead of cry. "The people back home thought I was lucky to come to this paradise. I'm glad they can't see me now," she thought to herself, almost wishing she were back in the security of her little Minnesota apartment.

A white Porsche came to a screeching halt in front of her. She stepped back still searching for a cab then she heard the harsh voice demand, "Get in." Startled, she looked at the driver and her heart sank as she saw the bronze face and the thick black hair.

"No thanks," she said crisply. "I'm waiting for a cab," and she started to walk away.

"You're not likely to find one around here," he yelled at her, "and besides they are scarce when it rains." Then in a caring tone he added,

"I'll be glad to take you to your hotel."

Caught in the dilemma, April reluctantly got in the sports car apologizing for her appearance. With her shoulders hunched over, feeling vulnerable, she slid onto the black leather upholstery and flippantly said, "I suppose this will cost me extra."

Derick laughed at the idea. "No, I don't mix business and pleasure," he said as he grinned at her. April couldn't help but wonder what lay behind his strange enigmatic exterior.

"Working kinda late, weren't you?" he asked.

April hedged in her seat and said, "That shouldn't surprise you," turning to look out her side of the window.

Though she was thankful for the ride to the hotel, April couldn't forget the hurt of the afternoon. Perhaps it was his chauvinistic attitude she resented. She began to see a trend: he thought women were inferior and needed his help. A stubborn streak ran through April and she was determined to show him she could make it on her own.

Breaking the uneasy silence, she offered a compliment, "This sure is a nice car."

"Thanks," he replied shifting gears to show off its speed. "Have you had dinner yet?"

Skeptical of his question, April paused and then quietly said, "No."

"Here's a good restaurant and it's close to your hotel," he remarked pointing to a red brick building. "It's also quite reasonable."

"Thanks. But I'm quite capable of finding my own restaurants," she heard herself retort with an abruptness that was close to rudeness.

As the car swung into the driveway of her hotel, April said, "Thanks. I hope I haven't inconvenienced you." Her words were polite but sharp.

As soon as the door was closed behind her, Derick drove away like white lightning. April could only assume he had actually gone out of his way for her. Puzzled she thought maybe it eased his conscience to occasionally do a nice gesture. Maybe he slept better at night.

April hurried to her room to change her wet clothes then down to the coffee shop for dinner. As she was seated alone in a booth near the cash register, she couldn't help but wonder what it would have been like to be seated across the table from Derick.

He was maddening, infuriating, and unpredictable, yet she had to admit, feud as she might with him, she wanted to be with him. Temporary craziness seemed to overtake her. For the first time in her life, loneliness seemed to engulf her. She quickly finished her meal and sought out the solitude of her little room.

Chapter 3

The next day, watching the dawn envelop the sleepy city, April went for a long walk along the beach. It wasn't just the exercise she wanted, but she needed the sea's ministry. She needed the wind to blow the cobwebs from her mind so she could think more clearly. The sea reminded her of the vastness of God's love and the tide's ebb and flow of His dependability. As she walked, she became determined not to let yesterday's failure defeat her. She silently prayed for God's guidance for that day.

As April entered the gallery and was greeted by Tessie, her faced glowed, causing the Oriental girl to say, "Looks like a good night's sleep did wonders for you."

"It's a new day and new beginnings. I'm looking on the positive side—things couldn't possibly be worse than yesterday," she remarked as she headed to her office to once again pore over the paperwork. She was absorbed in her work when a light tapping on the door stunned her. She looked up as Tessie whispered, "Can you come out and talk with a customer. He's especially interested in the Conroy watercolor." Her enthusiasm was bubbling over since that was a work of art selling for an exorbitant price.

April quietly slipped out and stood by the gentleman admiring the huge painting. "It's impressive, isn't it?" she said in a voice slightly above a whisper. Taken aback by the intrusion of his silence, the man peered down at her. "Yes, indeed. The colors are exquisite. My wife has been redecorating our house and I think this is exactly what she is looking for to hang above the sofa. The effect is most interesting." He pondered the idea as he gazed into the painting.

"I'd like my wife to see this," he decided. "Would you hold it for me until tomorrow when I can bring her in?"

Eager to sell the painting, but not wanting to be a high-pressure saleswoman, April, trying to keep her calm, used a sales technique she had

learned from her uncle. "Sir, the only real way
to see if the colors are right is to take it home and
try it. If you're not happy with it, you can return
it within 14 days." Intuition led her to believe,
from the way the man was admiring the painting,
that he loved it and most likely would not return
it. Besides, if he paid for it, she could use his
money for two weeks and worry about refunding
it when the time came. With quick calculation she
realized the profit would enable her to pay the
rent. She hoped her eagerness to sell it wasn't too
overwhelming to the client.

"Wouldn't it be great to surprise your wife with
it?" April prodded the gentleman.

"Why, yes, yes, it would." The man thoughtfully considered the idea. "Okay, I'll take it.
Would you please have it delivered to my home
by 4 P.M. today?"

Hardly able to contain herself with joy, April
wrote out the paperwork and the gentleman wrote
out his check. No sooner had she heard the tinkl-
ing of the bell signaling the man was out the door
than she let out a whoop of cheer. She kissed the
yellow check and grabbed Tessie and together they
danced with glee in the middle of the floor.
"Wow, we can pay the rent. I can't believe it,"
April chanted.

Her enthusiasm was contagious. "I'm on my
way to the bank," she shouted with glee. Grab-

bing her purse and rushing out the door she yelled back at Tessie. "I'll get a bite to eat while I'm out but I'll hurry back since I can't wait to hand over a check to our despicable landlord," she gloated.

The lines were long at the bank but April didn't seem to mind. She patiently waited her turn to make the deposit and felt so lighthearted she wanted to skip out. She felt the pressure was off now that the back rent would be paid. Oh, sure, there were other bills but they were smaller.

After lunch, April practically pranced back to the gallery. As she entered, she saw Tessie in deep conversation with a young man. "Oh, here's April now," Tessie said looking from the gentleman's portfolio. "Show her your work."

April came to take a look at his oil paintings spread out on the chrome and glass table. "How delightful," she burst out spontaneously as she noticed the playfulness expressed in the children's faces on the canvases. The colors were vivid in reds, yellows, blues, and greens. The man obviously had studied his subjects and was able to capture their innocence in a manner that was neither stilted nor poised.

"We're not in a position to purchase these," April told him, "but I would love to take them on consignment if you'll agree. I'm sure we can sell them." The artist left five of his best works at the gallery and after he left April immediately put them on display. Now her lagging confidence was so high that she couldn't wait to face Derick Donovan.

"I'll be right back," she called out to Tessie as grinning from ear to ear she nearly flew to the elevator. It was after 3 P.M. and she rode alone to the eleventh floor with her head held high watching the numbers of each floor light up. She laughed to herself realizing she hadn't called for an appointment. It was possible she wouldn't get to see him personally but she secretly hoped she could. What was there about her that made him think she wasn't a businesswoman? At times the job did seem overwhelming but now she was convinced more than ever she would prove to him she could do the job. Did he think blondes just looked for fun? Well, she'd show him. If the art gallery didn't succeed it wouldn't be because she didn't give it her all.

As she opened the door to Suite #1107, there was Derick dictating a hasty note to his secretary. "And sign that 'Sincerely Yours,' et cetera, et cetera," he said to her and then turned to face April. Seeing his beguiling smile made her cockiness melt away. There was something magnetic about the man. He was like the dawn coming up thunder. "And what can I do for you today, young lady?"

"It's more like what I can do for you," April smuggly told him. "Here's the past two months' rent," she said, thrusting the check in his hand. "And from here on out, you'll have it on time."

"What did you do, rob a bank?" he inquired with exaggerated astonishment. "I really didn't expect you to have the money so soon."

"I'm sure you didn't," she answered brightly, casting her head demurely down and then lifting it to gaze into his eyes. "I hope this will prove to you that women can be shrewd business people." She let the words sink in and then added, "I really must get back to work."

The secretary was busy answering the phones as Derick walked April to the elevator. "By the way," he questioned her, "where did you have dinner last night?"

Puzzled by his question, April shrugged her shoulders and said, "Why, just in the coffee shop at the hotel."

Disgust crossed his face as he went on, "But I told you about several great restaurants near your hotel. Why didn't you try one?"

April obliged him by saying, "And if you remember, Mr. Donovan, I told you I didn't like going to swanky places alone."

"Tonight I'm cooking dinner at my place. Would you come?" The change in his attitude was like a car shifting gears.

April wasn't sure she heard him correctly. To conceal her nervousness as she unconsciously played with her dangling bracelets, she laughingly asked, "What are you fixing?"

"Does it matter?" he quipped with a snarl on his face.

"No, not really," she meekly replied looking into his puzzling brown eyes.

"Good, then it's settled," he sighed relieved he hadn't received a rejection. "I'll pick you up at seven."

"Yes, sure, uh, that will be fine," April stammered, still dazed at the change in events. Unable to comprehend what she had just agreed to, and confused by her emotions, April was glad she could escape into the elevator.

As she rode to the ground floor, her mind was in a chaotic state. The man was so unsettling. "What have I done?" she lamented. "I hardly know the man and I'm going to be alone with him at his place. It doesn't make sense. One moment he can be so rude and arrogant and the next he's cooking dinner for me." Her mind was a mumble-jumble of questions as she slowly made her way back to the gallery.

April decided against telling Tessie of her dinner date. After hearing her say such nasty things about Derick, Tessie would probably think it strange she was now going to his place. April could hardly believe it herself. Since she couldn't keep her mind on her work she decided to leave at 5:15 P.M.

"I think I'll go a little early tonight," April said to her assistant. "Would you mind locking up?"

"Not at all. Have a nice evening," Tessie said, continuing her work.

"If she only knew," April groaned forcing herself to keep the secret.

Back in her hotel room, April scanned her temporary closet, uncertain what to wear. Jeans were far too casual and her office dresses seemed too staid. She finally decided on her mauve pants with its matching halter top. The soft fabric made her feel so feminine. As she was applying fresh make-up and wondering where Derick lived, the shrill sound of the telephone interrupted her thoughts. It was still another hour before he was to arrive.

Answering, she heard the familar southern drawl, "How close are you to being ready?"

Confused by his sudden change in plans, "I can be ready in just a few minutes."

"Good. I'll be there shortly and will give you a call from the lobby." His manner was brisk and to the point.

When the phone rang again, April knew it would be Derick and her heart began to pound fiercly. "Oh, heart be still," she whispered to herself as she placed her hand over the beating organ, as if that would slow it down.

As she approached him in the lobby, she felt his eyes scanning her body. His only comment was, "Hmm, you look nice." A feeling of euphoria swept across her.

Gently he took her arm and steered her to his car. He politely opened the door for her and then walked around to the driver's side and slid behind the wheel.

With a mischievous grin, he looked sideways at her and said, "You'll never know if I finished my work early or if I got anxious to see you."

At a loss for words, April smiled sweetly at him hoping her inward excitement at his comment wasn't revealed in her face.

The ride was short. Derick drove the Porsche into an underground parking structure of a high-rise building. He pulled into his assigned spot, helped April from the car, briskly escorted her to the elevator, and together they rode in silence to the 12th floor.

"This way," he muttered and motioned April to follow as they left the elevator. April's eyes grew wide with curiosity as she stepped into the attractive bachelor pad. The carpet was carmel colored and an overpowering brown and silver foil wallpaper marked the entrance way. A compatible paper was carried through into the small kitchen.

He ushered April into the living room and said, "Make yourself at home," and with a sweep of his arm indicated for her to sit on the plush brown suede sofa. "I hope you won't mind if I take a quick shower," he continued matter-of-factly as he exited.

April sank into the sofa stroking the soft fabric. She looked around the room which was obviously decorated by a professional interior designer. Glass end tables trimmed in polished brass flanked the sofa. They held matching brass lamps. The massive glass coffee table held current business magazines. April thumbed through one as she waited. Not interested in the subject matter, she walked to the sliding glass doors and marveled at the view from the lanai. To the right she could see the busy intersection of traffic but straight ahead she watched the peaceful scene of boats coming into the yacht harbor. She loved the warm feeling that enveloped her. Then she walked to the massive bookcase to browse through the titles. The range was varied as she read titles of novels, how-to books, and business economics. She was surprised to see among his collection a leather-bound Bible. At the end of his bookcase was a stereo unit and record albums. April flipped through his records and noticed his taste was rather conservative.

"Sorry if I disappoint you," he said reappearing surprising April, "I don't have any rock music."

"Actually, I see we have a common taste in music," she replied noticing he was now barefoot wearing white shorts and a white short sleeve shirt.

April followed as he went into the kitchen and began assembling ingredients for their dinner. "Is there anything I can do to help?" she asked.

"Just keep the cook company," he joked letting his dark eyes search her.

April stood in the doorway as he began taking food out of the refrigerator. He unwrapped two pork chops, seasoned them, put them into a pan and then into the oven. He searched the fridge for the makings of a tossed salad.

As he washed the lettuce, tomatoes, mushrooms, and sprouts, April delighted in watching him work. "You must enjoy cooking," she said.

"Yup," he responded, "it's a kind of therapy for me after a hard day at the office."

After the salad was made, he stuck it back into the refrigerator and began preparing blueberry muffins. He was very organized and tidy as he worked in his kitchen. As April watched the business tycoon prepare his gourmet meal, she smothered an urge to give him a hug around the waist.

"I'll bet your relatives like to vacation in Hawaii," April casually mentioned.

"No, I'm an only child and I haven't seen my parents in over ten years." He kept his attention focused on his kitchen duties as he talked. "I never felt they loved me. As a kid I was always a loner. I worked my way through college so was never able to take part in many social activities. When I graduated from college, I drove my car across the country putting my past behind me." He revealed his inner hurts without bitterness.

It was hard for April to comprehend that upbringing—it was so different from her happy, loving family.

Then to change the subject, he said, "There is something you can do. Here, set the table," and he handed her plain white china plates and brown tweed placemats. April obediently took the dishes and went into the tiny dining room. She carefully folded the beige linen napkins and placed the forks on top.

As she set the table in silence, her heart felt a kinship for this man. He had given her the idea life was a breeze, but now she knew deep down there were resentments and hurts as he worked his way up the corporate ladder. Her mind clicked back to the first time they met. He had claimed he didn't have time for marriage and a family. Now it made sense to her. Rather than risk being loved, he poured his energies into his work. "For the time I'm in Honolulu, I hope we can at least be friends," April hopefully thought to herself.

April went back into the kitchen as Derick was taking the pork chops from the oven. "Hmm, smells delicious," she complimented him.

Together they carried the food into the dining room. He pulled out a chair and indicated April was to sit there. He lit the candle in the center of the table and then walked away to dim the lights. April watched as he changed the music on the stereo to soft dinner music, then came to stand beside her.

He gently bent to her height and said, "We have a little custom here in Honolulu," and gently kissed her on the lips. April's heart fluttered and she responded to his kiss. His moist lips lightly touched hers again.

Then he took his seat across the table from her. April strained to contain herself. "Can this be the same man who said he'd charge interest on my overdue rent to make me learn management skills?" she debated with herself.

He began passing the food to her and she mechanically filled her plate even though she didn't feel hungry. The chemistry was certainly right, making their small talk a silken experience. April asked about his travels. He talked freely of adventures in India, Taiwan, and Thailand. He chatted about visiting politicians in London and having dinner with a prince in Saudia Arabia.

"You must have some fabulous photographs?" April inserted as she daintily wiped her mouth with her napkin.

"No, I don't even own a camera," he said reaching for a second helping of salad.

"And I suppose you don't even buy souvenirs of your travels?" she questioned, looking around the room and noticing the lack of artwork, sculpture, or even knick-knacks.

"Nope, it's a waste of time and money," he reflected.

Then the conversation drifted back to his college days. He related that after he got his master's degree from a leading California university, he gained experience working for an auditing firm.

"When you set your goals," he challenged her, "you don't set them for third class but aim for first. Then you can always back down."

She thoughtfully considered what he said and then thinking of her work at the gallery remarked, "But isn't it degrading and humiliating if you don't reach your goals?"

"There are no failures unless they stop you and bother you."

Conversation flowed easily and April felt like she was talking with an old friend. The bond was strong. April found herself engrossed with his life. Questions just tumbled out.

"Hey, that's enough about me," he said, his

accent oozing like melted butter. "I want to know more about you." April was stunned at this statement. Most men she knew only wanted their egos fed and didn't care about her opinions. She found it hard to talk about herself but tried to answer his probing questions.

As April finished her last bite, she laid down her knife and fork and said, "That was an absolutely fabulous meal." She noticed Derick was flattered by her open admiration.

"It's more comfortable on the sofa," Derick said pushing back his chair. April followed him and sat next to him. The view from the sliding glass door had changed to the blackness of night with stars twinkling overhead and in the distance a small sliver of the moon.

She turned to smile at him as his hand slid around her shoulder and he tenderly began caressing her bare arm. He pulled her to himself and kissed her on the neck. A warm sensation rushed through her body as she ran her fingers through his thick black hair. Gentle kisses became more passionate as he held her tight.

"You will spend the night," he said, more as a statement than a question.

"No, I won't!" she emphatically told him.

"What do you mean?" he demanded, forcibly holding her shoulders. "We have more chemistry going than Dupont."

Taking a deep breath and barely able to look at him she said, "That's enough."

"Oh, don't tell me," he mocked as he let loose of her, "you're only a tease."

Embarrassed that she had gotten carried away with his display of affection, she hesitantly told him, "I'm just an old-fashioned girl with old-fashioned values."

"Oh, come now," he harrassed her, "don't tell me you don't play around?"

Tears welled up in her eyes as she stared out the window. "I don't intend to be a Barbie doll you play with when you feel like it, then toss aside when you're finished."

He shook his head and sighed, thoroughly confused by her turn against him. "I know you're used to having everything and everyone you want," she continued. "But this is one time you're going to have to settle for less than your goal. For once in your life, Mr. Donovan, you're going to know failure." She blurted out the harsh words.

"So what's the big deal?" He shrugged his shoulders. "If it feels right, go for it. That's my philosophy."

"The Bible has always been my guideline."

"The Bible," he mocked her. "Oh, you've gone religious on me. I haven't heard anyone talk about the Bible since I was a kid and went to Sunday school."

The shocked look on her face forced him to continue. "Believe it or not, I grew up going to church every Sunday in Kentucky. I've read all about the Ten Commandments. A lot of 'thou shall not's' if you ask me. But what has that got to do with now—the 20th century?"

"The Bible is relevant today. God's laws were given in love because He cares about us and knows what is best for us. Since He is the One who created sex, it stands to reason that He understands even better than we do why it can never be satisfying outside of marriage."

The silence was awkward. Finally he looked at her and mumbled, "Come on. It's late. I better get you back to your hotel before my animal desires get the best of me."

April stood up and smoothed out the wrinkles from her pant suit. She fluffed up her hair, wishing she could make herself invisible. Her heart ached as she realized their short friendship was over. He had the power to make her feel miserable although deep down she knew she was right to stand by her convictions.

Since deflating his ego, he now seemed eager to get rid of her. He held open the condo door for her exit.

Timidly, she said, "I hope I haven't completely ruined your evening."

"No," was his only comment.

As the elevator plunged downward, April dared to ask, "Can we still be friends?"

"What's the use?" he sneered, looking at the floor.

He strode briskly to his car and opened the door for April. He revved up the engine and the sleek car roared to life.

The streets of Honolulu were void of traffic in the late night hour and Derick lost no time in getting her back to her hotel. April realized any attempt at conversation was useless. His sweet-then-sour attitude puzzled her. As he drove she studied his profile and fought back tears, feeling an emptiness inside her. She longed to reach out and touch him but knew she would be misunderstood. Once he looked in her direction but was silent. Had her refusal of his advances been that much of a setback to his male ego? Was it the first time he had been defeated?

The brakes squealed as the car came to a halt in front of the hotel. He made no move to open her car door.

Hesitantly she said, "It was a delicious meal," avoiding any mention of the after-dinner events. "Thanks," she softly said as she lowered her eyes and started to close the door.

"April," Derick haltingly said, then waited until she looked at him. "You know, my kind is a dime a dozen, but you're one in a million!"

Chapter 4

April gently closed the car door. Her thoughts were in a turmoil. Had she heard him correctly? His words had a caring, docile sound to them. Maybe deep down he did respect her stand. She knew she was right. She walked into her hotel feeling a wave of loneliness and rejection. Why? she asked herself. Why did their short relationship have to end this way? The question kept ringing in her ears.

The first thing she noticed as she entered her tiny room was the red light on the telephone blinking, indicating there was a message. She dialed the front desk and was disappointed to learn she had missed a call from Uncle David. Oh, dear, she worried, I hope it wasn't anything urgent. It's too late to call him back tonight.

Slipping into her nightgown, she washed off the makeup from her creamy complexion. Her mind was a jumble of questions. How could one man be so inconsistent in his moods? Why did Derick have to ruin what could have been a perfect relationship? The icy stare he gave her as he drove her home came back to haunt her. Would he ever want to see her again? But then what did he mean when he said, "You're one in a million"? Did he really admire her for daring to be different?

She tossed and turned in her kingsize bed but each time she was about to sleep her mind would rev up and present a new set of torments.

After more than an hour of sleeplessness, she got up for a drink of water. She bowed her head against the bathroom mirror and prayed, "Dear God, I know I did the right thing but why do I feel so miserable? I feel like I lost," she anguished. "That's not the way it's supposed to be. Why do I care about Derick? Help me see him as a friend—nothing more. Amen."

She climbed back into bed, but her restless mind would not calm down. The harder she tried to sleep, the more awake she became. It was nearly dawn when fatigue overtook her. It seemed like only minutes before her faithful alarm sounded.

Unable to push aside the mixed emotions of last night, she mechanically dressed for work. The light beige makeup refused to hide the dark circles under her eyes.

As she walked into the gallery, she self-consciously felt Tessie look at her and presumed she noticed her puffy eyes. No questions were asked.

She was glad for all the work piled on her desk. At least it would keep her distracted from thinking of Derick for hours.

The shrill ring of the telephone interrupted her work. "Uncle David," she nearly screamed, "Is everything all right?" she asked, excited to hear his voice.

"Everything is fine on this end," he answered. "I hope it is on your side of the Pacific. You were out kinda late last night, weren't you? I hope you're not working late," he said in a concerned voice.

"Umm, yes, I got your message too late to call you back. I'm sorry but..." she stammered, not wanting to tell him about Derick. "I had dinner with a...a friend," she said hoping she wasn't fibbing calling Derick a friend.

"I don't want to pry," Uncle David teased, "but I hope it was a tall, handsome gentleman."

"Actually, he's tall and handsome but I'm not sure you'd call him a gentleman," April said, reminded of their value conflict. "Anyway, I'm sure you didn't call just to check up on me," she nervously laughed as she played with the telephone cord.

"No," he assured her, "My artist friend, T.J. Richard, just talked to a friend of his who now lives in Honolulu. She's a very prominent lady who could probably give you a lot of help on the pre-opening benefit. She has done lots of charity events and knows all the right people to invite. T.J. talked with her yesterday and she suggested getting a committee of women to help sponsor the charity." Uncle David's tone was joyous as he continued. "She suggested to T.J. that the proceeds could go to establish an art scholarship for students."

April caught his enthusiasm as he talked. "Her name is Mona Gates and her phone number is 362-4782. She's expecting a call from you, according to T.J. I think it would be a good idea if you could get her and a couple of ladies together for lunch and discuss some ideas. Is there enough money in petty cash to treat them?" he asked.

"Yes, things are starting to look up. We sold a painting that had been around for a long time and that paid the back rent. I really believe the gallery has good possibilities. We'll just take it one day at a time."

"April, I appreciate the job you are doing there. I know it isn't easy but I have confidence in you."

Uncle David's words of assurance were bolstering.

"Thanks," April replied. "I'm really glad you bought this gallery. Otherwise I may never have seen this beautiful paradise."

"You're enjoying your stay then? It hasn't been all work?"

"You wouldn't believe the marine blue water, the fine white sand, the swaying palm trees, and weather that is always 75 degrees," April tantalized her uncle. "How could one not enjoy it?"

"Remember," her uncle reassured her, "we're just a phone call away if you need anything."

"Thanks a million, Uncle David, and tell everyone 'Hello' for me."

"I will. Talk to you later, dear."

"Bye," April said weakly into the phone. It was comforting to hear a friendly voice and to know Uncle David had faith in her.

She turned back to her paperwork and then a few minutes later remembered she promised to call Mona right away. She felt a little insecure calling this prominent woman asking for her help. But it had to be done.

Knowing Mrs. Gates was a socialite, April didn't expect her to answer personally so was taken aback when she heard the cheery "Hello" on the other end of the line.

"Mrs. Gates, this is April Anderson of the Gottery Art Gallery and I understand you are a friend of one of our artists—T.J. Richard."

"Oh, yes," Mrs. Gates chimed in before April could go on, "We've known him for years and I'm so excited to see his work finally selling. It will be good to see him again. It's been years. He mentioned he would be here for a benefit you're planning. So I said if I could be of any help.... My women's club sponsors scholarship funds so I suggested we start a scholarship program for art students. Naturally, it should be named after T.J. However, if you have other plans, I don't want to interfere," she rambled on.

April sighed with relief to find such a sympathetic volunteer. "Uncle David said perhaps you could get three or four key women together and we could have a luncheon meeting. Would that be possible?"

"That's a great idea, dear. Which day would be convenient for you?" Mona asked.

"Just about any time," April said while glancing through her desk calendar, noticing she didn't have any appointments penciled in. "Perhaps the sooner the better since we don't have a lot of time."

"Okay, let's make it Friday," Mona arranged. "That will give me time to contact the ladies. Let's see...shall we meet at 12 noon at the Summit Restaurant? I'll make the reservations. I am most anxious to see T.J.'s latest works."

"I'm sure you will be pleased with them, Mrs. Gates," April replied, feeling at ease with this enthusiastic woman.

"Please call me Mona," she bubbled. "All my friends do."

"Okay, Mona, I'll see you at 12 sharp on Friday. Thanks so much for your willingness to help with the benefit. I've had so many other distractions that I haven't been able to give it much attention. Bye for now."

"Bye, dear," came the cheery response.

April's spirits soared as she hung up the phone. This was just the boost she needed.

She turned back to her paperwork when Tessie came bounding in hurriedly exclaiming, "A huge shipment of oil paintings just arrived from Hong Kong. Do you know anything about them?" she questioned April. "The truck is out back wanting to unload them."

"Let's go see," April said in a quandry over the latest crisis as she got up from her desk. The men were unloading a heavy crate from the back of the truck. They set the wooden crate down and one of the men handed some papers to April.

"Would you sign here please, ma'am," and he indicated by putting an X on the line.

"Wait a minute," she declared. "I don't know anything about this."

"It's a shipment of 40 paintings from Hong

Kong. Here's the invoice," he said, handing her the multiple copies in yellow, blue, and white. "They've just been cleared through customs. This is Gottery Gallery, isn't it? These were ordered by a Mr. Chow."

"Oh, no," moaned April. "He no longer works here."

"Hey, we're just delivering them," the driver said shrugging his shoulders.

"Well, put them here," April feebly replied pointing to the back room, uncertain how she would pay for them.

"Do you want us to open the crate, lady?" asked the assistant as he walked to the truck to find his crowbar.

"Yes, please," April responded, curious as to the contents.

With one quick rip, the top came off the crate and April noticed each painting was individually wrapped with protective paper.

April began unwrapping one of the large paintings as Tessie watched dumbfounded.

"I can't sell this kind of artwork," April said. "It would lower the quality of the gallery. This is the type of work that sells along the park on Sunday afternoons."

"Maybe some of them can be used," Tessie said hopefully as the two continued to unwrap the paintings.

"It's not that they are bad," April said reflectively. "They are just not imaginative. It looks like they were mass-produced." Thinking out loud she continued, "I wonder how much we have to pay for them." She reached for the invoices. "Well, they're not too expensive, but that doesn't mean we can afford them. And we hardly have the money to ship them back."

"Just what I needed," April retorted sarcastically. "I only get over one hurdle and then it's another setback."

"You'll think of something," Tessie assured her. "You always do."

April smiled at the Oriental girl, feeling comforted by her compassionate understanding.

"We better get back to work," April said as she headed toward her office.

When the morning's mail arrived, Tessie took it to April who glanced through it, purposely avoiding the bills. Her mind was in turmoil as she wondered what to do with the Hong Kong paintings. She picked up the new art dealer's magazine and began scanning the pages. One bold headline caught her eye—"Easy Steps to Rent Your Overstocked Artwork."

"That's it!" she shouted jumping from her chair. "Tessie, Tessie, I've got it!"

Her sudden yelling frightened Tessie who came running into her office.

"What is it?" the girl asked breathlessly.

"It's so obvious. I can't imagine why I didn't think of it earlier. We can *rent* the paintings we received from Hong Kong. I'll bet there are many people who would love to have one of these in their house but can't afford to buy one. Let's rent them out for a month and then the people can bring them back for an exchange if they want, or they can keep it longer. They don't have an investment in the artwork but they can still enjoy the benefit of an original painting. What do you think?" She spoke in a voice that was contagious with enthusiasm.

"It would work on the same principle as a lending library. We'll print up some flyers and hand them out at shopping centers. Even some of the hotels would probably like to rotate their paintings. I think it will work," she said, mentally working out the details. "Not only could we bring in a little extra money, but we wouldn't have to worry about storing the paintings."

Tessie said, "I think it will work. I have some friends who might be interested in the idea. I'll be with them today and start passing the word."

"We could keep the gallery open for lending between 6 and 8 P.M. That way it wouldn't interfere with our regular clientele," April said.

"Good idea!" said Tessie. "I'll start working on a flyer."

It was late afternooon when April realized how sleepy she was. Each day seemed to be packed with problems but she tackled them one by one. However, she was beginning to feel the strain. If her life had been busy before, it was hectic now.

During the day she had tried to forget her disturbing encounter with Derick. Is it just infatuation that makes him linger in my mind, she wondered. Fuzziness clouded her thoughts. Since she would keep the gallery open until 8 P.M. when the lending of paintings program began next week, she justified leaving early today. She filled her briefcase with important papers as she grabbed her purse and closed her office door. She decided the walk back to the hotel might clear her mind.

The walk in the afternoon sun felt good. Exhaustion set in when she reached her room. She threw back the covers on the bed, slipped off her shoes, turned on the TV, and fell asleep. The shrill sound of the telephone awakened her with a start. "Hello," she muttered into the wrong end of the receiver.

"Hope I'm not disturbing you, dear," came the pleasant voice. "This is Mona. I called at the gallery but the girl said you had left and she gave me your number."

"Oh, that's perfectly all right, Mona," April said forcing the sleep out of her voice.

"I called my friend Lynn to invite her to our

luncheon meeting on Friday but she mentioned she and Terry have to fly to the mainland tomorrow. Terry's mother is very ill," she said, wandering from the main topic of conversation. "She asked if I knew of anyone who might housesit on such a short notice. I thought of you immediately. I know how dreary it can be cooped up in a hotel room. The Martins will be away at least two weeks and maybe longer. Would you be interested?" Mona asked.

"Why, yes," April emphatically replied, not believing her good fortune.

"You will love their house," Mona went on. "It's just a short drive from town. I'm sure you could use their car too. If you don't have any plans for this evening, I would be glad to drive you out there to meet the Martins."

Quick to answer, April said, "I can be ready any time it's convenient with you."

"I'll pick you up in an hour," Mona replied.

"Thanks so much," April said, "I look forward to meeting you. Call my room and I'll meet you in the lobby." She hung up the phone and let out a "Whoopee" as she raced to her closet to change her clothes.

Chapter 5

*P*unctually an hour later, the phone rang. "I'm in the lobby," Mona cheerfully sang out.

"I'll be right down," April said, and then in order for Mona to recognize her, she added, "I'll be wearing a white eyelet blouse with a big ruffle and pastel yellow slacks. I'll also be flashing a wide grin." The thought of leaving her tiny hotel room excited her.

Mona was all that April expected her to be. "Any friend of T.J.'s is a friend of mine," she said throwing her tanned arms around April. April assessed Mona as a lady with a healthy glow who looked like she had just won a close tennis match. Her long dark brunette hair was brushed away from her face and her dark eyes revealed warmth. She had an air of sophistication about her, yet she seemed very unpretentious.

"Let's go," she said to April, steering her into the direction of her parked car. "I can't wait for you to meet the Martins and see their house. It sure beats living in a hotel room," she said, gesturing at the high-rise building as they drove away.

April enjoyed the scenery as Mona steered the Cadillac out of the Waikiki district, past Diamond Head and into a plush residential area.

Noticing April's thrill at seeing the sights, Mona said, "You can't spend all your time working. We'll have to find a way to get you to Pearl Harbor and to the Punchbowl. There's more to Hawaii than just Waikiki Beach."

April's eyes widened and her mouth dropped open as Mona pulled into a circular driveway. "Is this it?" she asked in amazement. A huge white wooden house was set among lush green grass surrounded by a white picket fence. White columns stood on each side of the double doors with the stained glass windows.

As they walked to the door, April's knees felt weak. She was in awe as they climbed the brick steps and Mona rang the doorbell.

They were greeted by Lynn. April felt an empathy with this lady when she saw the strain and concern in her eyes. The uncertainty of her mother-in-law's health gave her a worried look.

Mona made the introductions and Lynn politely invited them in. April tried to conceal her astonishment at the luxury of the home. The foyer was plush with white carpeting and a magnificient crystal chandelier which was also reflected in the huge gold-framed mirror. A splashy wallpaper was carried through into the living room where a blend of old-world pieces were combined with contemporary accents.

"We're in a tizzy trying to get everything done so we can leave tomorrow morning for Iowa," Lynn explained, engrossed in the problems of her mother-in-law. "Terry's mother just had a heart attack, so we must get there right away. Please excuse me if I seem rushed," Lynn apologized.

"Oh, I understand," April assured her.

"Mona said you might be interested in housesitting for us. We always like to have someone here while we're away. There's really nothing you have to do except water the houseplants and pick up the newspapers. The gardener comes on Saturdays, the pool man on Fridays, and the maid cleans on Tuesdays and Saturdays. The freezer is stocked and I'm sure you'll find everything you need, that is if you're willing to stay," she added, not wanting to take April for granted.

"Oh, I'd love to," April quickly replied.

"Well, then, let me show you around," Lynn said, leading the way from the living room. "Just feel free to make yourself at home here. Invite your friends over." Before she could go on Mona interrupted. "April has been busy working and hasn't had time to meet many people, have you, dear?" April felt uncomfortable but nodded her head as Mona went on. "I could always call Stanley. He enjoys showing pretty girls around."

Mona kept talking as they toured. "Stanley's my husband's nephew. A brilliant boy. He works at Bailey & Green Law Firm. Graduated with honors from Harvard. I'll be sure to call him," she said, jotting a note in her daily reminder. April didn't have a choice in the matter.

"This is the kitchen," Lynn said as they approached the spacious room with its island work area. The leaded glass windows overlooked the backyard. Copper pots hung from the ceiling and green plants thrived in the windowbox. April noticed a microwave oven and the latest appliances. Wouldn't it be fun to fix a romantic dinner for two, April wistfully dreamed. Derick naturally came to mind. Then she remembered he didn't even want to be friends.

Lynn continued the tour with April and Mona following behind. "Here's our den," she said, switching on the light and revealing a room with warm woods and rich colors surrounding a collection of literature, artwork, and memorabilia. The leather wingback chair looked inviting as April visualized herself curling up with a gothic novel.

"The bedrooms are upstairs," Lynn said mounting the spiral staircase. The master bedroom was gray, brown, and black with all the latest electronic equipment. It was livened by the contrasting golds and reds of Chinese accessories.

"This room probably suits you best," said Lynn entering the guest bedroom. April fell in love with the four-poster bed and lace canopy. The walls were covered with Laura Ashley fabrics in pale pinks and soft grays. The traditional mahogany furniture added elegance to the romantic hideaway.

A man's voice yelled from downstairs. "Lynn, telephone..."

"Oh, excuse me," Lynn said nervously before dashing away. "Things have been so hectic leaving on the spur of the moment. If you are willing to stay here, Terry will give you the keys and you can move in anytime tomorrow. We leave early."

"I'd love to stay," April gushed. "I've never seen such a beautiful house."

"Good," Lynn said looking relieved. "We'll be away at least two weeks and if it's any longer we'll call you. Terry," she yelled, "give April the keys." Then she hurried to talk on the phone.

Terry met April and Mona downstairs. He handed April a keychain explaining, "This is for the front door, this one opens the back door. This is for the cabana and here are the car keys for the BMW. It's parked in the garage now. Any questions?"

Overwhelmed, April couldn't think of any. "I promise to take good care of everything."

"We'll leave phone numbers where we can be reached," Terry said. "If there are any problems, feel free to call us. And enjoy your stay," he added with a smile.

Sensing the uncompleted tasks that lay ahead for the Martins, Mona and April hastily said their good-byes.

On their drive back to the city, April basked in the warm glow that saturated the sea and the sky, filling every crevice with golden color. She watched as two young girls in muumuus skipped along on the sidewalk.

"I can't believe it," April burst forth. "I feel like I am in Disneyland in that house. It's so fabulous. This is almost too good to be true. Thanks, Mona, for thinking of me. I appreciate it so much."

"It will benefit you both," Mona said, thrilled that the young girl was so pleased. "Lynn's lucky too to find someone on such short notice."

April's mind was far away as they drove back

to the hotel. She couldn't wait for the opportunity to sort through the cookbooks, finding a perfect menu for two. She visualized laughter and talking as she brought a scrumtuous salad from the refrigerator, pretending it had been no effort at all to make. But her dreams kept including Derick.

"Stanley is probably sailing this weekend," April heard Mona say. "But I'll call him Monday," she enthusiastically told her. "He really is a nice guy."

Maybe he's the one who will taste my chateaubriand, she thought to herself. "I'll look forward to meeting him," April politely replied, hoping he was as dashing as Mona indicated. Maybe he can make me forget Derick, she rationalized. After all, he is a lawyer and does have his own sailboat.

"I wish I could help you move in," Mona continued, "but we're going to Maui for the weekend. I leave after the luncheon meeting."

"That's no problem," April assured her. "I can take a taxi."

The car came to a stop in front of April's hotel. "Thanks for everything, Mona. I'll see you at the Summit tomorrow at noon," she said climbing out of the car.

April forgot she was tired. She was too keyed up for rest or dinner. I think I'll walk to the shopping center, she mused to herself.

The walk was pleasant in the balmy night air. The sun was setting, making for a picturesque scene as she strolled past the yacht harbor.

At the Ala Moana Shopping complex, April decided to look for a new dress to wear to the luncheon. If all the ladies are as sophisticated as Mona and Lynn, I need a dress with a bit more class, she convinced herself.

She browsed through the racks of dresses at the large department store but didn't find anything suitable. Continuing her walk down the mall, she stopped at several of the smaller specialty shops, finally noticing a "sale" sign in an exclusive-looking store. A silver-haired saleswoman asked, "May I help you, honey?"

April cringed at being called "honey" by the stranger but sweetly said, "I would like to look at some daytime dresses."

"This way, please," the clerk said as April followed.

As April slid the hangers down the rack, a dusty pink dress with puffy sleeves caught her attention. It was a lightweight cotton dress with a flared skirt and high neckline. As she held it up to her, searching for a mirror, the saleslady intruded, "That would look stunning on you. The color is good with your sunstreaked hair and this wide belt will accent your tiny waist." Her persuasive powers reminded April of her Aunt Ethel.

The salesclerk ushered April to the dressing room. April slipped on the dress, then stood back to get the full effect in the three-way mirror. This is it, she reflected to herself. This will help boost my confidence at the luncheon with these wealthy women.

"I'll take it!" exclaimed April. "This is the first time I have ever bought the first thing I tried on. Things are going right for me today!"

April paid for the dress and left the store feeling exuberant with her purchase. After hanging up her new dress back in the hotel room, she slipped into her nightgown and was ready for a good night's sleep.

She knelt beside her bed and prayed, "Dear God, thank You for the good day. I have so much to be thankful for...forgive me for not always putting You first in my life. Help me to be grateful when things are going well and not just turn to You when I need Your help. You've been so good to me...thank You for the opportunity and challenge of managing Gottery Gallery. Thank You for finding Mona and for the work she is doing for the benefit. And I'm so grateful for the chance to housesit in a house lovelier than I could have ever dreamed or imagined. Forgive me for being selfish and complaining when things haven't gone my way. Amen."

The next morning she awoke refreshed. She took one last look out the window from her lofty view, then finished packing her bags as she reflected on the duties of the day.

The bellman helped her get her bags into a taxi. She sat back to relax as the cab took her to Gottery Gallery.

As she was paying the fare, the familiar white Porsche came to a screeching halt beside the taxi. "You aren't giving up and going home, are you?" he jeered half mocking and half sympathetic.

"Not on your life," April snapped back giving him a smile. "Things are going too well for that!"

His puzzled look prompted her to go on, "I'm just moving to more plush accommodations." Without looking back, she entered the gallery feeling very confident in her new dusty pink dress.

The responsibilities of the gallery made the morning fly by. At 11:45 A.M. she dashed out leaving Tessie alone to manage the affairs. "I can't be late meeting these important ladies," she said running with her briefcase in hand.

The ladies were all seated when April arrived at the Summit promptly at 12 noon. Mona began the introductions. "This is Meg Daniels," she said as April shook hands with the plump woman dressed stylishly in a silk shirtwaist dress. "Her husband owns a printing company so we can get the invitations printed there," Mona explained, having most of the details of the benefit already worked out.

"And Stephanie Stevens knows a great caterer who I'm sure we can count on and she's fabulous at flower arranging. She always comes up with the best floral arrangements." April smiled at the lady in the blue and beige sundress revealing her tanned shoulders.

"Pat McDonald here," Mona continued, "has connections with the local newspapers and TV shows. She believes she can get T.J. on some talk shows. That will help promote the exhibition."

"Great," April said responding to the lady whose short cropped hair gave her a manish appearance. Her dress was more tailored than the others, suggesting she was a professional businesswoman.,

"You might be interested in knowing," Mona said, explaining a little bit more about Pat, "she owns an original Dali, not to mention a lot of signed and numbered lithographs."

"I'm especially proud of the new Toulouse-Lautrec I acquired. Maybe you know it?" she questioned April. "It's called 'Le Secret.' "

"That's fabulous. I'd love to see it sometime," April said, impressed with the lady's collection. "You must be proud to show it off."

The brunette, who appeared to be in her early forties, was brutally frank. "Goodness, I don't display my paintings. They're in a vault. I collect fine art, but not for the aesthetic value. Art, as I am sure you know," she emphasized the words, "is a great investment."

"Of course, it is," April defended herself. "But there's no reason why you can't enjoy it, too."

"I've learned to buy things when I see them, even if I have to borrow the money," Pat explained to April. "They'll be gone later, or the price will be doubled, tripled, or even quintupled."

April bristled at the idea. "I don't like to talk about art as an investment. I'm offended by that." April stood her ground.

"I love art," Pat said firmly. "I've collected nearly 20 pieces which I feel will go up in value. I've got a good eye for that sort of thing. Art is only as good as its worth."

"Not so," April blurted out, enraged over the woman's insensitivity to beauty. "Art is to be enjoyed, appreciated, and the only way to do that is to be able to see it often and admire the work, the hours of dedication the artist put into it and, and..." April was surprised at her boldness in telling this woman her feelings and was glad when Mona gently intervened.

"Ladies, there are two sides to everything."

April realized her cheeks were flushed. Pat had indeed roused her dander.

"It's obvious we don't agree," Pat condescendingly told April. "But nevertheless, I'm interested in T.J.'s work. I've seen the piece that Mona has and I believe one day it will be very valuable. I want to be able to collect his paintings while the prices are still down."

April felt humiliated. No one came to her rescue. Did they all agree with Pat? Or were they afraid to disagree with this strong woman?

The waiter brought their watercress salad as the topic of conversation turned to the details of the benefit. Hesitantly, and then with more enthusiasm, April began to tell about T.J.'s work. "He'll have 21 paintings with him," she explained. "They'll be on exhibit for ten days. However, the night before we would like to have a pre-opening benefit. Mona has suggested we use the proceeds to establish an art scholarship. Would that be agreeable to all?"

They nodded in agreement.

April continued, "It's been suggested the tickets be $25 each and we'll just serve light refreshments. The ideal date would be Sunday evening, three weeks away. Are there any questions?" she asked.

The waiter placed hot plates with chicken breasts, glazed carrots, and rice pilaf in front of each lady. The ladies asked several questions while they ate.

As they finished their strawberry tart and coffee, April talked, "I really believe you will be pleased with T.J.'s work. The serenity and colors of his art have a special appeal. His work has really caught on in many parts of the mainland."

April noticed Pat glancing at her watch so wasn't surprised when she said, "I must get back to the office. I'm looking forward to the benefit and you can count on me to publicize it." Her words were crisp as she stood to leave. "Thanks for the lunch. We'll be in touch. Bye."

"Bye," April said weakly, almost glad to see her leave.

When she was out of sight, Mona comforted her. "Don't worry about Pat. Her theories are quite different from the rest of us but she's a hard worker and you can count on her to get the job done."

April was relieved the other ladies seemed to understand, yet wondered why her own defenses were so riled by this money-hungry woman who only saw art as an investment.

It was nearly 3 P.M. when April returned to the gallery. These ladies are wonder-women, she thought to herself. With Mona heading the committee, she felt confident every detail was under control.

April worked at the gallery until 8 o'clock. Eager to get settled at the Martins', she called a cab. She was elated as the driver left her and her luggage at the front door. She located the key

Terry had told her would open the door and smiled with pleasure as she walked into the house, realizing it was home for the next few weeks.

Carrying her bags to the guest bedroom, she felt like royalty as she unpacked. April began hanging up dresses and putting away her lingerie when she heard cars in the driveway.

Her heart skipped a beat as she saw two squad cars. She froze as the policemen in their dark blue uniforms pried the windows. She heard a thump and a yell. "We're police officers. Is there anyone inside?"

Goosebumps rose on April's arms and her legs were shaky as she walked down the oak spiral staircase. Her knees were like jello as she held onto the bannister for support.

Two officers with their hands poised on the guns in their holsters waited for her at the bottom of the stairs.

The older officer asked kindly, "Lady, are you alone?"

"I...um, I thought so," April said her voice barely audible. "What happened?"

"Were you aware a security alarm was set off?" the policeman asked.

"No, I don't know anything about it," April answered innocently.

"What happened?"

"'That's what we want to know," said the

rookie with his sun-bleached hair. "Just who are you? And what are you doing here?" he demanded unsympathetically.

"I'm April Anderson. I'm housesitting for the Martins while they are away." She tried to sound convincing but her voice wavered.

"How did you get in?"

"I have a key, of course," April explained. 'I can show you."

"No need for that," the older officer replied. "But why didn't you turn off the alarm? Did you realize you didn't lock the front door?"

"I don't know about the alarm," she admitted and then her shock turned to horror at her carelessness. "I thought I had locked the door."

The rookie had walked back to the patrol car. He signaled the other squad car to leave, then began talking on his two-way radio.

April felt the need to explain her situation. "Terry's mother had a serious heart attack so the Martins left this morning for the mainland. It was only decided last night I would housesit and they were in a rush and really worried about Mrs. Martin's health. I guess they just forgot to tell me about the alarm."

The rookie rejoined his partner saying, "Headquarters have no identification on an April Anderson. We're going to have to take you down to the police station."

Fear permeated every inch of her body yet she knew she was innocent and there was nothing to worry about.

"It's just a matter of routine," the older officer said as he escorted April to the police car. "There's nothing to worry about. I'm sure there's just some mix up."

"Can I get my purse," April asked.

"I'll get it," the younger officer gruffly stated. "Where is it?" Hearing April's instructions, he walked into the house and shortly returned with it under his arm.

April nervously rubbed her hands together. She was humiliated and scared as she sat alone in the backseat of the squad car. The older man drove as the rookie talked on the two-way.

"It's all just a mistake. You'll see," she tried to explain.

"I'm sure it is," the driver tried to comfort her. "We'll just take you to headquarters and then if you can have someone come down and identify you, you'll be free to leave."

April's mind was spinning in a circle of indecision of whom to call. She had never thought to write down Tessie's phone number. Derick would probably belittle her for not knowing enough to turn off the alarm. Mona had been so kind and gracious. I hate to bother her, April thought, but she is the logical one to call.

"Is there anyone you can call to identify you?" the young officer inquired.

"Yes," April calmly stated, "I can call...." Then she remembered Mona had said they were going to Maui for the weekend.

At that moment she realized she had no choice. She would have to call Derick. Her heart sank. "I can call Derick Donovan," she said, hesitantly.

"You know him?" the young officer stared at her in astonishment. "You mean the business tycoon who is building all of the new high-rise office complexes?" Then he chuckled before going on, "If you know him, you're doing all right!" His voice had a lilt about it.

Devastated that she would have to ask for Derick's help, April realized she would have to swallow her pride. She knew he would gloat over the opportunity to rescue her from this embarrassing predicament.

As the officers helped her into the police station, she silently prayed, "Lord, I'm asking you to help me out of another mess."

Chapter 6

*A*pril felt the stares of the other officers as she entered the station. This is just like the police stories on TV, she mused to herself as her knees trembled. She expected to be finger-printed and held behind bars until Derick could arrive. The kindly officer dispelled her fears. "If Mr. Donovan will come down," he explained, "you'll be free to leave." He motioned her to sit by one of the wooden desks and handed her the telephone.

She was relieved it was that simple. No bail or bonds. "We're sorry to do this to you," he went on, "but it's routine. If we had known you were a friend of Mr. Donovan's though, we could have called him from the house.''

April was taken by surprise as she learned of Derick's importance in the community. She tried to steady her hand as she dialed his office number. It rang once, twice, three times and then a masculine voice answered, "Hello.''

Hearing the familiar twang in his greeting crumbled April's desire to remain cool and aloof. "Derick,'' she blurted out, "I'm sorry to bother you but I need your help.'' The urgency in her tone revealed her helplessness.

"I'm at police headquarters. I accidentally tripped off the alarm system where I'm housesitting. They want...I mean I need someone to identify me.'' The words stammered but she went on. "Would you be able to come here?'' She bit on the words knowing he was probably gloating on her dependence of him to get her out of this situation.

"Sure,'' came his amiable response.

April's mood perked up as she heard him say, "I'll be there in 10 minutes. Don't worry,'' he guaranteed her, "everything will be okay.''

The minutes seemed like eternity as April waited for Derick's arrival at police headquarters. She anxiously watched the door for this familiar gait.

Her heart began to pound when she saw him walk briskly into the station. He carried himself as someone who is used to having his way. The sight of him brought an unwilling smile to her lips. She moved to stand beside him. Her voice was high-pitched and her words ran together. "Derick, please tell them that I am housesitting for the Martins and that I run Gottery Gallery."

"Officers," he said directing his attention to the two uniformed men, "I'm sure there is some mistake. This is April Anderson. She's a businesswoman who has recently come to our city. There's no reason why you can't trust her and I will personally be responsible for her actions," he said in his authoritative style.

"We're sorry for the inconvenience, Mr. Donovan, but we were just doing our duty," the rookie said justifying his behavior. "You are free to go now," he said almost apologetically to April.

April regained her composure and some measure of poise as Derick grasped her hand and led her to his car.

"It was so awful," her voice sounded low. She took a deep breath, settling into Derick's car.

"Where to?" he inquired as he slid into the driver's seat.

"The Martins," she calmly told him giving him the address.

Neither talked much as they drove to the prestigious neighborhood. She wondered what he was thinking about now.

"A penny for your thoughts?" he finally asked glancing in her direction.

"What?" she asked in mock concern. "You're a financier and that's all you'll offer me?"

They both laughed and April began to feel more at ease. She was relieved he hadn't poked fun at her failure to turn off the alarm system.

He drove the Porsche into the driveway and came around to open April's door. "I better teach you how to use the alarm system."

"I really do appreciate all you did," April shyly said. "Have you had dinner?"

"No." He came to the point immediately. "Do you think you could find something to satisfy my hunger pains?"

"I'll try," April said as they walked to the kitchen. This wasn't the way she had intended her dinner party for two to be. She searched the refrigerator but nothing seemed appealing. "How about a salad?" she suggested and then quickly dispelled that idea as she held up the limp lettuce.

"That's okay," he comforted her. "I really should be going. I have a 6 A.M. breakfast meeting tomorrow."

He put his finger beneath her chin and forced her to look up at him. "Will you be all right alone?" he asked gently.

"Yes," she answered feeling a faint flush of excitement.

He put his arms around her as her head rested on his shoulder. Enjoying the warmth of his bear hug, she hesitated moving. He represented a pillar of strength. He brushed strands of hair from her face and tenderly kissed her gently.

She cherished the moment and then spoke softly. "Derick, I'm really indebted to you. And it's embarrassing that I can't return the favor by fixing you dinner. Will you take a rain check?" Pleased that it worked out so naturally to invite him to dinner, she added, "I really am a good cook."

"Sure," he drawled and lowered his head and she felt his lips upon her own.

Taken aback by his amorous mood, April felt her pulse quicken. She released herself from his embrace and asked, "Could you come to dinner Tuesday night?"

"Thanks," he smiled at her, "but I have to work late. I'm getting ready for a quick trip to Hong Kong."

Her heart raced as she realized how much she enjoyed his affection. "But you have to eat," April insisted. "Would you let me bring dinner to your office? I could fix a picnic," she enthusiastically offered.

"It's a deal," he concluded with a mischievous grin. "But remember, real men don't eat quiche."

"Oh, the ego of your species...."

"Are you sure you'll be okay now?" he pressed her.

"I'm fine. Really I am." she assured him. "Thanks, Derick, for coming to my rescue," she said out of genuine gratitude as she walked with him to the door.

"Always ready to help a damsel in distress," he teased.

She met his eyes and encountered something questioning and wistful.

"Good night," he said bending to kiss her again.

Her breath was quick and her knees were weak after he left. Her wildest dreams wouldn't have revealed him so chivalrous. Maybe he just needed to be needed.

She went back into the kitchen to search the cupboards for the cookbooks. She discovered a good supply and heaped them on the breakfast nook. She thumbed through them, looking for the perfect picnic menu. It had to be special.

The next day April slept late. The strain of the events the last few days had taken its toll on her body. She was glad for the opportunity to linger over black coffee as she read the morning newspaper. At noon she drove the red BMW into the city. She carefully parked in the spot assigned to the gallery. Her eyes automatically searched for Derick's Porsche. His parking place was empty.

His meeting must have been elsewhere she decided.

On the way home that day, she stopped at the supermarket. She not only needed to stock the refrigerator for herself but wanted to pick up the groceries for her picnic.

She looked forward to the evening alone. After unpacking her three bags of groceries, she enjoyed a leisurely meal. Then she settled into the big leather chair in the den with a good book which kept her totally absorbed until after midnight. She yawned and crept upstairs to her bedroom.

On Sunday morning she checked the yellow pages of the telephone directory to locate a nearby church. The tall steeple on the white wooden structure reminded her of her church back home. The people graciously welcomed their visitor. April slid into a back pew and joined in singing the familiar hymns. Pastor Andrews radiated a gentle spirit as he spoke from the text of Philippians 4:13. "I can do all things through Christ which strengtheneth me." April listened attentively as he spoke of how God often uses people who seem inadequate to accomplish a big task. "His power shows up best in weak people," the minister said. He cited the example of how God used young David with his five stones to slay the giant Goliath. David's confidence was in the Lord.

The rest of the day was hers to do as she pleased. She donned her multicolored bathing suit, found a quiet spot on the white sand, and listened to the pounding surf. This is the life, she mused as she spread out her beach towel and lay down watching the whipped cream clouds float by. Satisfied with her tan after several hours, April packed up her belongings into the beach bag and drove home. She needed the time to organize Tuesday night's elaborate picnic.

She discovered a wicker picnic basket that perfectly suited her needs. From the linen closet, she produced a small red and white checkered tablecloth and two white linen napkins. She laid them aside with the red candle she had purchased.

Absorbed in her work on Monday, the day advanced quickly. She didn't mind working late. In fact, she was curious to see if anyone would respond to the thousands of flyers that had been distributed, advertising their art rental program.

Her confidence began to build when a number of people came by to look at the paintings. She assigned four on loan that night.

As the clients left, April locked the door and breathed a sigh of relief. The jarring ring of the telephone disturbed her silence. Who could be calling at this hour, she wondered as she hurried to answer the phone.

"Is this April Anderson?" the male voice asked.

"Yes," April replied cautiously.

"This is Stanley," the voice rang out. "Stanley Blacker. Mona gave me your phone number. She asked if I would give you the grand tour of our beautiful island," There was an eagerness to please in his tone.

"Oh, yes, yes." April said, vaguely remembering Mona had promised to have her nephew call.

"The city is spectacular by moonlight," the deep voice went on. "We could view the sights from the lofty mountaintops." April was uncertain whether he was trying to be poetic, romantic or both.

"Well, actually, I'm quite busy," April hunted for an excuse.

"Aunt Mona says you haven't begun to see the city yet. We wouldn't want you to go back home not having explored every corner," he persisted. "I'd like to show you around."

"That's very kind, Stanley," April said. Not wanting Stanley to feel like he was being used as at tour guide, she added, "But you really don't have to. I have seen quite a bit of the city."

"But I like meeting new people and making new friends," he persevered.

April sighed but hoped Stanley didn't sense her boredom. She was too excited about her dinner date with Derick to think of another man.

"How about tomorrow night?" he requested.

"No, I have other plans," she said refusing to elaborate.

"Then let's make it Wednesday," he urged.

"I have to work late," she said wishing he could take the hint.

"Friday night then."

"Okay," she agreed, feeling she owed it to Mona to at least meet her nephew. Maybe it would be good to take some time to see the sights and balance her absorption with work and Derick.

The next day she found her mind continuously daydreaming of Derick and the picnic she was planning. She kept nervously glancing at her watch wishing the time would fly.

After a hasty "Good night" to Tessie, she dashed home. There were a lot of last minute preparations for her dinner. After the wicker basket was packed to the brim, she picked the most beautiful white rose she could find in the garden and tucked it in the corner of the basket.

She hurried to change her clothes. Her white slacks and short sleeve white shirt looked crisp against her skin which still had the tint of pink from Sunday's sit in the sun. She added a wide red belt and red earrings. Dabbing her favorite perfume behind her ears, she ran down the oak staircase, pausing to look at herself in the mirror. Feeling absolutely sure of herself for the first time in over a week, she proudly picked up the basket and headed for the car.

The butterflies in her stomach began to flutter as she pulled into the underground parking of Derick's building. There's no use being nervous she tried to tell herself. We're just having a quick picnic dinner. That's all. What was there about him that sent her head spinning? Was it his style or his status in the world?

All of his staff were gone when April arrived. "Hello," she timidly said entering the empty reception area. "Derick," she said as she gently knocked on his office door.

He opened it and grinned as he saw her. "The caterer has arrived," he teased. "Little Red Riding Hood in white. May I help you with your basket?" he asked, taking the heavy load from her arms.

"I've heard the key to success is diversification," she joked. "So I thought dinner should come to you."

"Diversifying is one thing, but diversion is another," he quipped back with a gleam in his eye.

"Umm, smells good," he said winking at her as he set the basket on the coffee table.

"Let's eat on the floor," April suggested spreading the tablecloth out. "At least there won't be any ants at this picnic," she laughed. Unpacking the basket, the rose was set in a bud vase in the center of the cloth with the candle beside it.

"You outdid yourself," Derick said truly pleased with the effort April had expended.

As she laid out the plates, the crystal glasses, the linen napkins, and silverware, Derick stared in amazement. "You didn't forget anything, did you?"

"Actually, I did," she confessed. "Do you have any matches?"

He searched his desk and found a partially used matchbook from a swanky restaurant. On his way back to April, he stopped to dim the office lights. Then he eased his large frame to a cross-legged position on the floor and reached across to light the candle.

April filled Derick's plate with honey-baked chicken, potato salad, deviled eggs and tomato slivers. She noticed his eyes light up as she served him a homemade corn muffin.

"Fit for a king," Derick said taking the plate from April. "This sure beats a late night dinner at Coco's," he said referring to the 24-hour coffee shop.

She reveled in his praise.

"Do you always work late?" April quizzed him.

"Most often," Derick answered. "I love my work. It's the most important thing in my life."

"But don't you have other interests?"

"You might say I'm married to my work. I'm really happy with what I'm doing."

"What you think will bring you happinesss is not always what it seems," April interjected. "You have to keep working toward your goals but you can't let it be your idol."

"I have set some high goals for myself," Derick said reflectively. "Maybe it's a drive I got from childhood that I have to prove to myself that I can accomplish something significant. I'm really not sure," he said thoughtfully.

"Well you certainly are making some lasting contributions," she said respectfully.

"I'm really excited about the project my partner Pat and I are developing on the Big Island," he said with pride in his voice. "We've got a few problems to work out. It's been difficult locating new homes for the low income people living on the property we bought. But as soon as we find homes for three more, we can begin groundbreaking. I have a few details to work out on the financial package. That's why I'm going to Hong Kong this weekend." He smiled as he explained.

April felt important as Derick confided his business anxieties with her. She sensed his compassion when he spoke of relocating the people from their existing homes. An overwhelming sense of pride that she was spending time with this bachelor awakened in her a hope of romantic involvement.

"That was delicious," he took the last bite.

"I hope you saved room for dessert," she said reaching for the fresh strawberries. She dipped one into sour cream and brown sugar and then playfully stuck it in his mouth.

"You really are something special," he said, his voice smooth. Then he pulled her close to himself.

April was chagrined at the surge of warmth that invaded her body as Derick held her tight.

"You ought to come to Hong Kong with me," he invited.

"Are you crazy?" she laughed.

"No, I'm serious," he said loosening his grasp of her, "Why not? I'm leaving early Saturday morning. I will meet with the bankers on Monday and we could be back Tuesday morning before the gallery opens. Come with me?" he urged.

"I can't believe it," she replied in total shock. "I've never been out of the country before and you want me to fly to Hong Kong for the weekend."

"On Sunday night we could go to The Peninsula for dinner. It's my favorite restaurant on the waterfront. It's so romantic. Then on Monday you could shop while I conduct my business. You'd love Hong Kong. It's like one giant China-town," he said trying to convince her to come.

"There's no way I could afford it," she replied.

"You don't think I would expect a lady I invited to pay her own way, do you?"

Flattered she answered, 'But I've got a gallery to run.''

"You would only be away on Monday," he was quick to dispell her doubts. "And you said things were going well," he reminded her.

Her mind whirled with thoughts. Surely Uncle David wouldn't mind her taking a day off. After all, he would want her to take advantage of this opportunity. Maybe I could visit some galleries there and get some ideas she reasoned.

"Where would we stay?" she blurted out.

"Now that's what you're really worried about," he teased. "You're afraid that I'll tempt you beyond what you're able to handle and that there's no escape." he said, loosely paraphrasing a well-known Bible quotation.

"Well, that is a consideration," she said, feeling the color rise in her cheeks.

"You can't blame a guy for trying. I have a little apartment there."

As she looked at him blankly he said, "You're staring. Is it fear or fascination?"

She relaxed, laughed and then realized he may have taken her reaction as a positive answer. He gathered her in his arms and kissed her. Lost in their world, not until the door opened and they heard footsteps did their kissing stop.

"Am I seeing things?" a woman's deep voice sharply demanded.

Derick, taken aback by the intrusion, combed his fingers through his hair, sat up straight and said, "We've just finished dinner."

"That's some finale," the woman replied.

April, whose back was to the intruder, let the color drain from her face before turning away. When she saw the woman, she felt a strange sensation in the pit of her stomach.

Derick was on his feet as the embarrassment seeped away and a look of annoyance took its place. "Pat, this is April. She brought a picnic," he made an attempt at a proper introduction. "Pat is my business partner," he added turning to April.

"Well, I do believe we've met," came Pat's icy answer. "We don't see eye to eye on art investments and I can see we certainly don't agree on office procedures." Her words were bitter.

"What brings you back to the office tonight?" Derick asked his associate.

"I forgot some important papers for the meeting tomorrow. When I saw the light under your door, I thought I would see how things are coming on our Hong Kong project. But I see you're using delay tactics." Her tone was flat.

"They are coming just fine," Derick said between clenched teeth. "Everything will be in top shape for the meeting tomorrow."

April, feeling like she had caused the rift, began

packing up the remains of the picnic. She stood to leave "I...I'd better be going now," she timidly said as she eased her way to the door.

"Good idea," Pat said sarcastically, eyes ablaze.

Pat followed April to the elevator. "Derick's time is far too valuable for picnics on the floor," Pat said, glaring intently at April.

Hostility had gradually replaced April's happiness. "Well, we, he...uh had to have dinner," April muttered. She was visibly shaken by the experience of being caught.

"It looked like more than that to me," Pat said, her accusation subtle though direct.

April could muster no words as she silently wished for the elevator to come.

The elevator doors opened and as she stepped in alone, she heard Pat say, "Just don't think you can succeed in coming between Derick and myself."

"I didn't intend..." April's voice trailed off as the elevator plunged downward.

Chapter 7

April drove along the coastal highway at a conservative speed. If her sight was a little blurry, it didn't seem to matter as the two lane road was virtually empty. What had Pat meant when she threatened, "Don't think you can succeed in coming between Derick and me?" Was she romantically involved with Derick? Or did she mean not to interfere with their business? Why didn't Derick defend her from Pat's harsh tongue? I guess I really don't mean anything to him, she argued with herself. But why did he ask me to go with him to Hong Kong?

One thing is for certain—Derick wasn't the

chauvinist April orginally thought. It had come as a shock that his partner was a woman. Maybe it's just that he didn't trust my business sense, April worried.

As she pulled into the driveway she was still wrestling with the questions in her mind. It was a chance of a lifetime—to go to Hong Kong. The excitement of visiting a foreign country overwhelmed her. Maybe I should go with Derick and prove to Pat she can't stop me, April connived as her evil nature surfaced. But would she be able to resist Derick's temptations? She felt powerless in his strong arms. April was suspicious of his intentions. Her thoughts churned, struggling with the choices. Imagine! A weekend in Hong Kong. She envisioned the glimmering lights of Kowloon reflected in the dark mirror of the harbor and the bargains she could find while shopping.

April's mind was still whirling as she undressed for bed. Why did Pat have to ruin everything? Or had she? Derick's emotions are not of care and concern, only of convenience. That night she buried her head in her pillow and softly cried until she fell asleep. Her emotions made no sense at all to her.

The next morning the shrill sound of her travel alarm woke her from a fitful night of sleep. She stretched as she sat up in bed and wondered if the invitation to Hong Kong had been only a dream.

Then she recalled the events of last night and knew she had to make a decision. It was a no-win situation. She took a deep breath and decided some day she would see Hong Kong—on her own.

The next two days flew by swiftly. Mona stopped by to show April the printed invitations and to leave a supply for her to hand address. There were calls to the caterers and the florists. Stephanie called with a progress report on her assignments for the benefit. A televison station requested an interview with T.J. and a radio station offered to do public service announcements telling about the scholarship fund.

April was pleased with the way plans for the benefit were falling in place. In just the short time she had been at the gallery, she noticed an improvement in business and was especially pleased with the rental program. Perhaps it wouldn't be long before the gallery would once again be in the black.

Several times April heard Derick's Porsche rev up from the parking structure and her heart would leap in anticipation of seeing him. He hadn't asked for her decision regarding Hong Kong. By now, maybe the offer was off. Then she became determined to let him know she had reached a decision—whether he wanted to know or not.

Friday morning she telephoned his office and the receptionist put her through. "Derick," she began, her voice high-pitched. 'I just want to let you know, I'm not going to Hong Kong with you.'' He was taken aback with her directness. ''But I appreciate your asking,'' she continued.

''Oh?'' he mumbled as if he had forgotten his invitation. ''Maybe another time.''

''I hope you have a good trip,'' she said.

''Oh, sure,'' he said, almost sounding puzzled. ''Good-bye.''

April felt relieved when she hung up. She knew deep down she had made the right choice although she regretted missing the opportunity to see Hong Kong.

April had almost forgotten her date with Stanley. Maybe he would take her mind off of Derick and the trip she had passed up. I'll bet Stanley doesn't have swaying moods like Derick, she thought to herself.

That night as she was brushing her hair, the doorbell rang. Stanley was early. April took a deep breath and hurried to the door. Stanley was tall, lean, and wearing a black and white plaid seersucker jacket with white polyester pants. His dark blond hair was receding but curls swirled around at his neck.

''Hi,'' she said sweetly hoping her disappointment wasn't obvious.

''Hi,'' he returned and thrust a small package into her hand. She took it and opened it exclaiming, "How thoughtful. I love perfume." She placed the bottle on the table in the foyer as she smiled at him. He seemed so uneasy as he awkwardly stood on one foot and then the other.

"Is there any special place you would like to go for dinner?" he asked politely as he pulled a list from his jacket pocket. "We could go to the Hyatt Regency, the Sheraton, or Top of Waikiki. I always like to let the girl choose the place," he added with a grin.

"That's very kind of you, Stanley," April placidly smiled. "But I really don't know places here, so tonight I'll let you choose."

"Okay," he said, putting his list back in his pocket. "We'll go the Hyatt Regency. Money's no object with me."

April stuffed her house keys into her purse, amused that Stanley felt he had to impress her. They walked to his car as April shivered at the possibility of accidentally running into Derick. She felt guilty when she compared the two men, but Stanley just lacked pizzazz.

As they drove into the city, Stanley began asking questions.

"Is this your first visit to Hawaii?"

"Yes," April answered.

"Where are you from?" the probing continued.

"Minneapolis."

"Do you have brothers and sisters?"

"No."

"Do you have any hobbies?"

"I play tennis," she continued. "Back home I do a lot of snow skiing in the winter. I enjoy museums and plays, too."

Realizing she must show some interest in him in order to keep the conversation flowing, she asked him the same question. "What are your hobbies, Stanley."

"I love to sail. I have my own boat. I used to do a lot of fishing but now that I'm a lawyer," he said with pride in his voice, "there isn't much time." He looked at her and smiled.

They arrived at the Regency and Stanley gently touched April's elbow, steering her into the posh restaurant. The evening can't end too quickly she bemoaned. Stanley is a nice guy but he just doesn't have the charisma of Derick. She winced as she realized she was comparing them again.

Stanley hadn't thought to make reservations. The maitre d' told them the wait would be one and a half hours. "We'll be back," Stanley said as he added his name to the waiting list.

"Let's walk around," Stanley suggested, attempting to hold April's hand. They walked to King's Alley where tiny white lights reminded April of Christmas decorations. They browsed in the shops looking at souvenirs. Stanley insisted on buying April a pastel pink T-shirt advertising

Honolulu. They watched lei sellers push their carts.

"How are things at the gallery?" Stanley started his barrage of questions again. "I was really impressed when my aunt said you were running it."

Not wanting to go into details, April simply stated, "Fine."

"Maybe next Sunday we could go to the art museum," Stanley eagerly asked.

"Well," April stammered looking for an excuse. "I really have a lot to do getting ready for the pre-opening benefit in just two weeks. I'd better not make any commitments." She smiled at him. He really is trying, she thought to herself. What had made the conversation with Derick so natural the first time they met?

"Okay," Stanley said, not ready to give up, "I'll call you later in the week."

They walked back to the restaurant and in just a few minutes the maitre d' seated them. The room was elegant, decorated in pinks and reds with white lattice work and green plants. The table was elaborately set with fine china, crystal, silver, and candles casting a warm glow. Fresh flowers gave an added touch of class.

The waiter handed them oversized menus. "Do you like lobster?" Stanley asked her.

"Why, yes," she answered and gulped when she noticed the price.

"We'll each have the lobster," he informed the waiter. "And don't forget the butter."

Stanley tried to say every bright and funny thing he knew, managing to drop into the conversation every achievement he had ever secured from Boy Scout badges to his grades at Harvard. Intent on impressing her, he flirted and flattered yet his manners were impeccable.

As they drove home, an idea seemed to cross Stanley's mind as he suddenly suggested, "Would you like to go for a moonlight stroll? We could walk through the park next to the beach?"

"Thank you," April said forcing a smile which she hoped wasn't beginning to look mechanical. "But I have a busy day tomorrow and really need to get home."

His disappointment showed but he brightly added, "Maybe you would like to go sailing next weekend?" She would have loved the opportunity to sail, but not with Stanley.

"I really have a lot of work to do getting ready for the pre-opening benefit," she again reminded him.

The Toyota came to a stop in front of April's temporary home. Stanley fumbled as he opened the car door for her and his nervousness was more apparent as he walked her to the door. She put the key in the door and turned to him, "Thanks for the nice dinner."

Once her words were out, he bent down and placed a wet kiss on her mouth. Before she could protest, he was down the steps and into his car.

Thank goodness it's over, she sighed. When do boys become men? Her mind drifted back to Derick—he was so suave and sophisticated and yet she felt so comfortable with him. Their conversations were as natural as granola.

There's no use daydreaming about him, she determinedly told herself as she tried to block him out of her mind.

Chapter 8

*O*n Saturday morning April fixed a
breakfast of pancakes with banana
syrup sprinkled with macadamia nuts. "Fit for
a king," she said out loud and it reminded her
of Derick. Why did all of her thoughts revolve
around him? He's on the airplane now, she mused,
thinking of the trip she had passed up.

After opening the gallery, she was delighted
when a client showed a positive interest in a
valuable painting. Things were certainly looking
up at the gallery. She decided it was time to adver-
tise for a permanent manager of the gallery. Perhaps if she found the right person soon she could

go back to Minneapolis after T.J.'s pre-opening benefit. With thousands of miles between us, it'll be much easier to forget Derick, she reckoned.

Sunday April again attended the neighborhood church. The Reverend Andrews was eager to introduce her to several people in the singles group. She appreciated his kindness and warmth to her.

In the late afternoon she took a scenic drive along the coast. She stopped at a lookout point and watched the emerald green water lap fiercely against the blackened lava, creating a blowhole. The rugged cliffs with their sheer drop to the fine white sand below, the coral reefs that were visible when the tide went out, the blue sky with its puffy white clouds would have been enough to send Monet rushing for his paint brush and palette.

She drove on to Kailua Bay and people-watched. Seeing the families enjoying a picnic, the high-schoolers playing a frantic game of volleyball, and lovers hand-in-hand beachcombing sent a sweep of loneliness through April.

Her mind taunted her with thoughts of Derick. Was he having dinner with someone else at his favorite restaurant? What was he doing right now in Hong Kong? Why am I spending so much time thinking about a man whose flaws are so apparent? I'm going to think of more positive things.

Monday passed quickly. No matter how busy she stayed during the day there were the agonizing long nights to get through. Derick would never sit around feeling sorry for himself, she reflected as she rattled around in the empty house. I refuse to get caught up in self-pity, she decided. I'm going to get dressed up and go to a nice restaurant. There was no reason why she shouldn't go alone, she convinced herself, aware that her ancient insecurities had disappeared.

She dressed in a simple black and white dress and slipped into her black pumps. The single strand of pearls around her neck gave her an air of sophistication. Wisps of her short blonde hair curled slightly around her face.

She felt an air of adventure as she drove into the city. Seeing the night lights and the many tourists strolling the sidewalks gave her a euphoric feeling. She drove through Waikiki and found a parking place near a western-looking steak house. She studied the menu outside before going in.

The hostess smiled cordially and then asked, "Will someone be joining you?"

"No, it's just me," she replied, noticing her words had ascended a full octave.

She led April to the back of the room next to where the swinging doors connected to the kitchen. She studied the menu even though she had already made up her mind what she wanted. She felt slightly uncomfortable, not knowing where to look. She played with the bayberry candle on the table and fingered the flower centerpiece. While waiting for the waiter, she began looking around the room. She saw tourists reveling in their first visit to the island and honeymooners gazing into each other's eyes.

Then her heart skipped a beat. Derick and Pat were entering the room. Pat was beaming as she held onto Derick's arm as the hostess ushered them to a table. Horrified, April didn't know whether to get up and sneak out when all at once, the waiter appeared wanting to take her order.

She stammered and couldn't remember what it was she wanted to eat. "I'll have the prime rib," she ordered "and, uh, I'll have the salad, no, the soup...with blue cheese."

"Ma'am, do you want the soup or salad?" the waiter asked annoyed.

She tried to quell the humiliation rising in her face. "Salad," she mumbled.

Maybe they won't see me, she thought. Perhaps I can exit while they're busy eating and talking. It looks like they are engrossed in a serious conversation. Maybe it's a business dinner, she tried to tell herself. Then she noticed the way Pat tenderly put her hand on Derick's arm. Even though he didn't return the endearing gesture, he seemed to be enjoying it by the look on his face.

Even though April was resigned to the fact Derick was not for her, it hurt to see him and Pat laughing and talking over dinner. Unconsciously, she realized she had not completely released her feelings for him.

Her salad arrived but her appetite disappeared. She went through the motions of eating but wished she were home devouring a frozen pizza and Twinkies.

April slyly looked in Pat and Derick's direction and noticed they were lingering over their meal. They hadn't spotted her yet so perhaps she could slip out without being seen. She paid her bill, mentally calculated a generous tip, then slid out of her chair.

She tried to avoid their table as she tiptoed along the wall heading toward the door. Then she heard his voice, "April?" There was no mistaking his drawl. "What are you doing here?"

Trapped, her eyes narrowed and she felt rooted to the spot, unable to think clearly. "What does one normally do in a restaurant?" and then immediately regretted her bitter attitude.

"But I thought you didn't like to dine alone," he reminded her. "Or aren't you alone?" he questioned as he looked around for a date.

"I'm alone," she flinched, without a smile.

Not wanting to be left out of the conversation, Pat said, "That's a brave thing for a young girl to do." April bristled at Pat's penchant for provoking her.

Refusing to let Pat have the upper hand, April turned to Derick and innocently pried, "How was your trip to Hong Kong? You only got back today, didn't you?"

"Yes." He noticed hostility building between the two women. "I got the job accomplished."

"I hope you had time for dinner at the Peninsula," April said, hoping Pat would realize she knew of his favorite romantic restaurant.

"He was there to work, dear," Pat insulted her.

"I really must be going," April said feeling that she was imposing. "It was nice seeing you." She almost choked on the words.

April hurried from the steak house. Why did seeing Derick with Pat upset her so? Pat hurt and humiliated her by making her feel inferior. She's a cold and devious woman who parades her power, April thought.

That night when she reached the safety of her home, the breeze felt good as she stood on the steps and looked into the twinkling stars.

"Lord, once and for all, I surrender to You my feelings for Derick. I am uncertain about them but please let me see him just as a friend. Forgive me for my hateful feelings toward Pat. If it's Your will, let me love her through You. Amen." She prayed, seeking absolution from the haunting bitterness of the past hour.

Chapter 9

The days seemed to blur together as April was absorbed in the many details of T.J.'s exhibition. There's more to organizing a benefit than I ever dreamed of, she sighed. What would I have done without Mona, she wondered. Her enthusiasm and organizational abilities were an inspiration to April. With the event less than a week away, the RSVPs were arriving daily.

Several articles had appeared in the daily newspapers promoting the event. April knew it was through Pat's efforts even though she hated to admit it. She conceded that the lady followed through on her commitments.

Mona and her husband had graciously extended invitations to Honolulu's elite for a garden party honoring T.J. It sounded magnificent to April. She hoped she would have time to shop for an appropriate dress. *Maybe if I grab a sandwich for lunch, I'll have time to go to the mall,* April mused late one morning.

She shouted her plans to Tessie, then slammed the gallery door behind her. The warm sunshine always felt good and the fresh sea air helped to clear her head as ideas and plans seemed to overwhelm her.

She walked briskly to the nearby deli. After looking over the menu, she peered through the glass counter at the array of corned beef, roast beef, and ham.

"I'll have a corned beef sandwich on rye," she told the man wiping his hands on a dirty apron.

"Make that two," drawled the familiar voice from behind. She turned and looked up into Derick's brown eyes. They appeared tired as evidenced by the wrinkles around them, but April noticed his lopsided grin, leaving her feeling vulnerable.

Before she could think of anything clever to say, he said, "Let's take our sandwiches to a favorite beach of mine. I like picnics." His eyes twinkled.

Quickly forgetting her shopping spree, April agreed.

They drove out of Waikiki and parked at an isolated beach. Only two other cars were parked nearby. Two young boys had cast their fishing lines into the green water and a few people walked along the shoreline.

April automatically picked up the brown paper bags containing the sandwiches and grabbed for the soft drinks with her other hand. From the trunk of his car, Derick produced a thread-bare dark green blanket.

As they walked closer to the surf, he said, "It's good to get away from the hubbub of the offices. Some days those phones can be wicked."

"I know what you mean," she agreed, thinking of all the work she had to finish before the pre-benefit opening.

"Things are going well at the gallery, aren't they?" he asked, observing that this month's rent had been paid on time.

Pleased that he had noticed, April remarked, "Yes, they are. I've put an ad in the paper for a manager. If I can find the right person, I'll be able to go back to Minneapolis soon."

"Haven't you liked it here?" His voice expressed concern.

"It's fabulous," April hastened to answer. "It's just that it's not home to me and you know what they say, 'There's no place like home!' "

"Home is wherever I am," Derick said

thoughtfully. "But I guess women have more of a nesting instinct."

Their time together was relaxed and friendly. There were no quarreling barbs between them today. April relished their moments together.

As the tide began to invade their territory, Derick stood up, "We'd better get back to work." He offered April a hand. When they reached the Porsche, April began looking around with a worried expression on her face.

"Derick, have you seen my purse?" she asked panic stricken.

"Did you have it with you while we were eating," he asked as he joined the search.

She tried to recall as she thought out loud. "I always take it with me but my hands were full with the sandwich bags and soft drinks that maybe I forgot my purse. But it's not like me to forget it. Was the car locked?"

Her face clouded with doubt as she searched the car for her purse. "No, I never lock it," Derick grunted. "Someone would have to be crazy to steal this car. It would be spotted too easily on the island," he said as he patted the streamlined white car.

"Then my purse has been stolen," April gasped as the realization sunk in. "All my money gone! I had a lot with the advance Uncle David gave me. My credit cards are gone too! I don't even have any blank checks. What am I going to do?" she frightfully asked as her hopes crashed against reality.

"Report it to the police," Derick said, slightly irritated at her carelessness.

"I didn't need to have this happen with all I have to do in the next few days," she moaned.

"Well, that was a stupid thing to do...leaving it in the car, I mean." Derick stripped her of dignity. "You ought to know kids hang around the beaches waiting for an opportunity to steal. Careless tourists are easy prey for quick cash."

Fighting back the tears, she blurted out, "I don't expect sympathy from you, Mr. Donovan, but I don't need a lecture pointing out my errors."

April was frustrated with her negligence but now the frustration turned to anger as she saw Derick's lack of concern. He knew she had a sheltered existence but now he was adding irresponsibility and immaturity to the list.

"Gosh, what am I going to do," she anguished. "I had nearly $550 with me. I hope Uncle David won't be furious."

Noticing her worried state, Derick sarcastically said, "I thought the Good Book said 'Money is the root of all evil.' You're not supposed to worry about it. Maybe you'll have blessings from above."

Straightening herself in the seat, she controlled

the tremor in her voice. "It's the *love* of money that is the root of all evil," she corrected him. Then she bit her tongue, refraining from adding, "You should know."

Any attempt at conversation seemed contrived. April's mind was plagued with a zillion worries. She was somewhat skeptical but knew she would have to call Uncle David and hoped he would be more understanding than Derick.

"Call Sergeant Henning," Derick instructed April as she got out of the car, "and file a claim. Sometimes the thieves just want the cold cash and they toss the other contents aside. Eventually the rest may get turned in." His telling her what to do was the crowning insult.

Yet his words "toss the contents aside," struck a cord in her mind. Maybe she could find her identification and other objects even if her money was gone. She was relieved to find she had left the Martins' key on her desk. It's worth a trip back out there, she decided. The work will wait, she thought as she rushed past the ringing phone and out the door.

She found the same beach and parked her car exactly in the same spot. Her mind teased her as she reflected on the laughter and chatter they had shared only moments earlier. Why did their encounters always have to end up with tension?

For 20 minutes she searched the sand and

brambles but saw no indication of her straw bag. She twisted her hands in an agony of despair, realizing the contents could be scattered miles down the road. Feeling dejected, she went back to the gallery and phoned the police.

April was irked at her carelessness. It was such a stupid thing to do. Her stomach felt like it was tied up in knots. In despair she pounded her fists on the desk and then realized she should notify Uncle David.

"Don't worry," he tried to comfort her. "We have insurance for things like this. I know it's an inconvenience to you but we'll take care of everything on this end. Is there enough money in petty cash until I can send you a check?"

"Yes," she replied, beginning to feel better.

"April, you're doing a great job there and I want you to know how much I appreciate it."

April's sagging confidence perked up after talking to her uncle and she delved into her work.

After dinner, April decided a swim might cure her restlessness. The night air was warm and the moon glowed overhead as she tested the pool temperature with her foot before gracefully diving in. Swimming the length of the pool, it felt so good to stretch out her long, lean legs. She didn't realize how tight her back muscles were until they began to relax after several laps. She swam until she was exhausted.

Chapter 10

April was puzzled as to who would be calling so early in the morning as she answered the phone.

"April, I'm so glad I caught you home," the voice sounded familiar but April couldn't immediately place it. "Terry's mother had another setback last night so we won't be coming home tomorrow as planned. Would you be able to stay at our house longer?" Lynn asked.

"I'd be delighted to stay, Lynn."

Their conversation was short. After hanging up, April let out a "Hallelujah. I don't have to move back to my tiny hotel room."

As April drove to work that day she found herself singing along with the radio. She remembered the first day of work at the gallery and how everything looked so bleak. By taking one day at a time, things had gradually changed for the better. Her day went smoothly with routine events.

She eagerly looked forward to T.J.s arrival the next day. She admired his work. He was much older than she, in fact old enough to be her father, yet she wasn't sure if the affection he always showed her was strictly fatherly. She put those doubts aside as she anticipated being his tour guide. It will be good to have a dinner companion, she contemplated.

As April left that evening, she noticed Derick's car was still in the garage. She couldn't help but admire him for his ambitions and goals. It was mind-boggling to realize a man of his age owned this building as well as several other high-rises in Honolulu. He had accomplished more in his 32 years than most men do in a lifetime. Pride began to swell up. Then she refused to let her emotions get carried away. This man didn't know the meaning of love, didn't care about learning it, and probably never would. Just remember that, she warned herself.

Saturday morning a gentle rain was falling. April hoped it would clear before T.J. arrived. She wanted to show him Honolullu at its finest.

By noon the sun was shining and there was not a cloud in the sky.

At nearly five o'clock, she decided to lock up. She wanted to freshen up before meeting T.J.'s plane. As she was unlocking her car in the garage, the rev of a Porsche began. She pretended not to notice but the squeal of the brakes near her car caused her to look up.

"Leaving a bit early, aren't you?" Derick questioned her.

"Yes," she conceded, "T.J. Richard is arriving tonight so I'm going to show him around." She gloated at the opportunity of letting Derick know she had a date for the evening. She purposely avoided telling him it was strictly a business arrangement.

"I suppose you have to work late," she sarcastically flung at him thinking it probably meant a cozy dinner with Pat.

He was amused at the irony in her voice. "I'm taking some work home but first I'm going to be a good Boy Scout and visit Pat in the hospital."

"Oh, I'm so sorry. What happened?"

"She was in an car accident last night. A drunken driver going the wrong way on a one-way street. Thank goodness neither was driving too fast."

"How seriously is she hurt?" April showed genuine concern.

"She has a slight concussion, fractured ribs, and a broken leg. They don't think there are any internal injuries. She's a fighter, so I don't imagine they'll keep her in the hospital too long."

April grimaced at the thought of Pat bedridden with a cast on her leg. She wondered how many people would visit her. Pat seemed to spend more time working than developing close relationships. People took advantage of her for the job she could do rather than liking her just for who she was. April remembered the comments from the ladies on the benefit committee.

"Please give her my regards," April said absentmindedly, and then more sincerely she added, "If she needs anything, please let me know."

"Okay," Derick said, "she probably needs visitors. See ya," he drawled before racing his car through the garage.

April slowly climbed into her car and wheeled it out of the parking structure. "She needs visitors" stuck in her mind. Surely she wouldn't want to see me, April rationalized. We haven't seen eye to eye on anything. It might upset her more if I visited her, she tried to convince herself. Besides Derick will be there this evening. Yet she couldn't imagine the busy businessman sitting in a hospital room very long.

The idea of visiting Pat in the hospital toyed with April's emotions. She suddenly remembered her prayer to God to let her love Pat through Him. Was He asking her to do that now? I'll send a nice card, she reasoned to herself, even flowers. But dear God, don't expect me to visit her tonight!

To further add to her misery, memories of her own hospital stay years earlier flooded her mind. The hours had seemed like eternity. Television was boring and reading monotonous. She had treasured every minute talking with her visitors.

She felt a sense of dread, something gnawing away at her as she changed clothes. I have to pick up T.J., she firmly maintained. Maybe tomorrow I can visit Pat.

As she drove to the airport, her heart was torn with anxieties as she rememberred her prayer to the Lord. If only I hadn't asked Him to love Pat through me, she groaned.

Checking the arrival schedule, she noticed T.J.'s plane was slightly delayed. She loved to watch people and it certainly was interesting here. People came in all sizes. There were pale tourists just arriving; others going home with deep tans; and there were the Polynesians with their dark skin and silky black hair. God really has a sense of imagination creating each individual differently. And to think He *loves* each one of them.

The thought struck home as April continued to study those around her. Pat was one of God's creations. If He loved Pat, why was it so hard for

April to love her. Maybe Pat had never known
of God's love. April knew nothing of her family
or close friends. Was Derick her only true friend?
If so, maybe that explains why she is so possessive
of him. In that moment, April knew what she had
to do. The struggle with her emotions ended. She
would visit Pat tonight at the hospital after she
had taken T.J. to his hotel.

The loudspeaker interrupted her thoughts as
she heard T.J.'s flight being called. People were
crowding the gate and April joined them. At last
she spotted T.J. He looked dashing in his khaki
pants and madras plaid shirt unbuttoned at the
neck. His slightly graying temples made him look
distinguished.

"April, darling," he oozed as she slipped a lei
around his neck and gently kissed him on the
cheek. "Hmm, I like this custom," he flirted.
"How are things going with the benefit?" he
quizzed her. "Did all my paintings arrive in good
condition?"

"Yes, they did," April assured him. "And
everything is just great, T.J. No need to worry."

"I knew you could do it, kid," he proudly said.
"Now, I'm all primed to see the Honolulu sights.
Where are we going first?" he asked flirtatiously.

"I'm afraid that will have to wait until tomorrow," April confessed, seeing the disappointed
look on his face. "Pat, one of the committee

members, was in an accident and I think it's important that I go by the hospital," April explained as they walked to the baggage claim area.

"What?" he asked in mock exaggeration. "You're going to let a famous artist sit in his hotel room alone on his first night in Hawaii? Not on your life!"

"But I have to," April weakly insisted, not wanting to have to give T.J. a long explanation. "Please understand," she begged.

T.J. sensed the urgency in her voice and quit pleading. "Well, a lady has got to do what a lady has got to," he said, turning the old maxim around.

"Tomorrow's all yours," she promised him.

As they drove into Waikiki, April was proud to point out the sights. The golden sun was setting behind the clouds, making it a postcard picture. "Would you like to go to a luau tomorrow?"

"Sounds great," T.J. answered. "You really know this city, don't you?" refusing to take his eyes from the car window. "I would like to see Pearl Harbor. Do you think we could put it on our agenda?"

"Great idea. I haven't been there myself." April was pleased she would have a companion to explore new territory.

"Here's your hotel," she said as they stopped in front of a beachfront high-rise. "Pretty classy," he said as he let out a low whistle. "Until tomorrow, dear one," and he blew her a kiss as she watched him take his luggage from the trunk.

As she drove away, she prayed, "Lord, I really believe this is what You want me to do. I can't love Pat in my own power. You'll have to do it through me. Let her see Your love, I pray. Amen."

As she walked slowly into the huge brick hospital, the strong medicinal smell in the corridor was a sharp contrast to the fresh outdoor air. She inquired at the information desk for Pat's room number. As she made her way to the elevator, she spotted a gift shop and bought a bunch of flowers.

She knew she risked rejection and the thought made her nervous. There's still time to back out, she thought as she rode the elevator to the fourth floor.

The door was slightly ajar to Room –412. April knocked gently. A hoarse voice said, "Yes?"

"Pat?" April questioned timidly and tiptoed into the tiny private room.

April flinched as she saw Pat in a white hospital gown lying motionless in the narrow bed. Her right leg was in a cast and it hung from a contraption strung over the bed. The television set was blaring and a half-eaten meal was on the bedside tray.

April noticed the look of surprise on Pat's face and then it turned to disgust as she said, "Derick has already left if you're looking for him." She turned her head away from April.

"Oh, no," April was quick to say, "I came to see you." She hesitated and then went on. "I brought these for you," forcing Pat to look in her direction.

"They're beautiful," Pat melted as April thrust them to her.

April glanced around the room and noticed hers were the only flowers—Derick hadn't bothered to bring any.

"Why don't you put them in this water pitcher?" Pat said handing April the green plastic container. The flowers added color to the almost lifeless room. April began nervously arranging the flowers and then set them in the windowsill.

"Have a seat," Pat skeptically said, pointing to the chair near the bed.

"Thanks," April said and then began the speech she had rehearsed. "I saw Derick in the garage this afternoon and he told me about your accident. I hope you're feeling better. If there is anything I can do you for...I mean, do you need any personal items from your house, or can I get you any magazines or books?" she asked. "I hope you'll feel you can count on me," she added.

Pat's brittle mood began to vanish. "That's

really sweet of you, April, but I can't think of anything now."

Puzzled by her unexpected visitor, Pat pointedly asked, "Derick said you were going out with T.J. tonight. You didn't change your plans because of me?" Pat was unable to comprehend that kind of concern.

"Well, yes," April shyly admitted. "We postponed our plans for sightseeing until tomorrow." Feeling uncomfortable with this kind of probing, she squirmed in her chair. "I know what it's like to be confined to a hospital. Three years ago when I spent a week in Minneapolis Memorial, it was my friends who got me through. We both know we view life differently but we have a right to disagree. Maybe we could learn from each other," she went on as Pat lay speechless.

April paused and looked away. Turning back to look at Pat, she thought she saw a tear. Was this worldy-wise woman softening?

Pat was quiet and April realized she would have to do most of the talking "I appreciate the work you've given to the pre-opening committee. I know T.J. will be pleased with the interview you set up for him at the *Star-Bulletin*."

When she ran out of things to say, April was astonished to find nearly a half hour had gone by. "I don't want to tire you and I think visiting hours are almost over," April said rising.

"Thanks for coming," Pat told her sincerely. "It meant a lot to me. I know being with T.J. would have been far more exciting, but you'll never know how much this meant to me."

By avoiding the two explosive subjects—Derick and art investments— the time had passed uneventfully.

"It was good for me, too," confessed April. "I hope you'll be out in time to attend the pre-opening benefit."

"I wouldn't miss it for anything," Pat affirmed. "This hospital stay is just a little inconvenience but I should be up and around on crutches in a few days."

"Bye," April said glowing as she left the tiny room. "Thanks, Lord," she whispered. "I think the visit did more good for me than it did for Pat. You taught me a lot about forgiving—it was a hard lesson but well worthwhile."

Chapter 11

*A*pril was still basking in last night's triumph when she met T.J. to begin their history lesson. They easily followed the signs pointing to Pearl Harbor.

They parked near the landing adjacent to the Halawa Gate and boarded one of the navy boats for the tour of the U.S.S. Arizona National Memorial. A white concrete and steel structure spanned the hull of the sunken ship. T.J. vividly remembered the December 7, 1941, incident and related his memories of that day. April only knew it from history books but was fascinated as their guide told them the details. They also visited the museum room where the names of those killed in the attack were engraved. It was a somber experience for the pair as they walked back to their car.

"Let's drive to the other side of the island," T.J. suggested eager to see all of Oahu.

"I'm game," April volunteered as she drove the car onto Kamehameha Highway headed toward the mountains. Several times they stopped the car at lookout points to get the full benefit of the lush green scenery.

Taking their shoes off, they walked along the beach at Haleiwa, letting the wet sand seep between their toes. The temperature was ideal and the warm breeze blew April's hair. They continued their sightseeing at Waimea Falls Park, viewing the much acclaimed waterfalls. As April drove the coast route back to Honolulu, she was caught up in the reverie of the day.

"You promised a luau tonight," T.J. interrupted her daydreaming. "We'd better hurry back."

The couple strolled onto the lush green grass of the Royal Hawaiian and heard the whisper of Waikiki's rolling surf and viewed Diamond Head in the distance.

They joined the line for the buffet feast. A long table decorated with a printed green and gold cotton tablecloth held exotic food. The basic fare was the kalua pig, a succulant porker which had been roasted for several hours in a rock-lined underground pit called an "imu." The pig had been wrapped in leaves from the taro plant and had a delicious smoked flavor. Also cooking in the imu were sweet potatoes, breadfruit, and green bananas. Another main dish called "lau lau" looked tempting. It was a special blend of beef and pork, herbs and fish, which had been wrapped in ti leaves and then steamed for hours. As the waiter explained the various dishes, April put a little of everything on her plate.

"What's a luau without poi?" April asked T.J. as she put a small amount of the pasty substance on her plate. "I understand you're supposed to eat it with your fingers," she commented, dipping her index finger into it. She puckered up her mouth. "Don't waste your hearty appetite on that. It's bland!"

With the food on their plates mounded high, they found empty chairs around a circular table. As they ate their meal, they found the other guests to be friendly as they exchanged greetings of names and hometowns.

After the sun had set, the torches surrounding the scenic area were ceremoniously lit. Chairs were turned around as the entertainment began.

"Aloha," the master of ceremonies greeted everyone. He wore tight white pants and his white shirt was open nearly to his waist. A pukka shell necklace was around his neck. "Welcome to our

enchanted islands," he began. Next he introduced
two young men who sang a Hawaiian medley and
played ukeleles. When they had finished, the applause was enthusiastic.

"Here's what you men have been waiting for,"
the emcee continued as he introduced the hula
girls. Three attractive ladies with black hair to
their waist, wearing green grass skirts and printed
halter tops accented with red leis, shimmied their
way on stage to the beat of the drums. They were
barefoot as they stepped lively and vigorously
worked their hips.

Next Tahitian and Somoan dancers set a lively
pace throughout the program which reached a
peak with an exciting fire dance. In the true spirit
of the aloha luaus, the dancers asked for volun-
teers from the audience. The women all urged
their husbands but none was willing. Three of the
dancers walked through the audience and coaxed
three men on stage. T.J. was one of them. The
people laughed and cheered as the men attempted
a stiff Hawaiian hula.

It was late when the program ended and April
left with T.J. "Whew, it's been quite a day,"
April told him as her mind was spinning with
memories.

Chapter 12

*T*he next day while April was with a client, Derick casually sauntered into the gallery. April's line of concentration wandered as she wondered what he could possibly want. He had never stopped by before. She watched as he quietly walked around the gallery, looking at the various pieces of sculpture and paintings. Then he stood back, obviously admiring a large oil painting, hands clasped behind his back.

When the client left, April ambled to where he stood and in mock tones asked, "Are you interested in that painting, Mr. Donovan?"

"Not really," he drawled as his intense brown

eyes searched her. "I just stopped by to see if you would like to go to Kona with me this afternoon."

Startled by his invitation, she questioned him "Just like that? You want me to drop everything and go to another island?" She relished in his surprise, but was flattered by his offer. Any feelings she had before of his infuriating behavior were immediately swept away.

"I hadn't planned on going," he continued, "but since Pat is still in the hospital, I need to negotiate on our property there. I just thought you might like to tag along. You could explore the island while I do my business. Then we could have an early dinner and be back here by 8:30 at the latest. How does that sound."

"Well, I don't, uh, well..."

"I think you would enjoy seeing the Big Island. It's quite different from Oahu," he persuaded. "It might be good for you to get away from the gallery for a few hours."

"That's a brilliant idea," she said nodding her head in approval. "I'd love to go along."

"Great," he replied, satisfied with his influential powers. "I'll stop by to pick you up at about 1:30 P.M."

April watched him walk out the door, then wondered why she agreed to go along. *I always want to be with him but we always end up at each other's throats. What kind of crush do I have on* this man that I put myself throught this every time? Then an odd thought whizzed by. Why does Derick keep asking me to accompany him? Could it be that he is interested in me?

Excitement of visiting the Big Island made the morning hours fly by. She left instructions with Tessie for the day's work. When she heard the roar of the Porsche, she hurried to the door and yelled back, "Tell T.J. I'll see him tomorrow."

"I must be going crazy," she smiled at Derick, "but everyone needs to step out of the routine once in a while. What's that famous phrase, 'Diversification is the key to success.' "

"I hope that's not the only reason you're going along," he bantered back.

"What time does our plane leave?" she asked, glancing at her gold watch.

"Whatever time we get there," he answered. "A plane can't leave without its pilot."

"You mean *you're* flying us?" her eyes were wide and animated.

"Yep. We're taking my plane. Are you going to change your mind?" he inquired with exaggerated astonishment.

"I'm not afraid," she retaliated as her heart gravitated toward this powerful man.

As he stepped onto the wing and helped April up the high step, they climbed into the cockpit and Derick cautiously studied the gauges.

"Here's the seatbelt," he handed the straps to April. As he did so, his hand brushed hers slightly and she felt a warm tingle.

Shortly the plane began taxiing down the runway. Unsure whether conversation would disturb him, April was silent causing Derick to finally ask. "You aren't scared, are you?"

"No," she laughed. "I'm just amazed. I had no idea you were a pilot. What other hidden talents do you possess?"

"I found that this saves a lot of time," he explained. "When we were building a condominium complex in Maui, I wasted a lot of time waiting for commercial flights."

April felt a faint flush of excitement when they were airborne. Derick was receiving instructions from the control tower as April peered out her window. Soon the little Cessna banked to the left and April saw the maze of hotels dotting the shoreline fade into the distance. She savored the view of Diamond Head as the plane climbed higher into the deep blue sky.

The thrill of flying with Derick left her giddy. She was swept away by her fantasy of how it would be if Derick could love her the way she deserved to be loved. She totally blocked Pat out of her mind as she basked in the enjoyment of the moment.

"How long will it take us to get to Kona?" she finally asked.

"About 40 minutes," he replied. "Unless we hit some strong winds."

After a few minutes of flying there wasn't much to see except the white caps of the dark green Pacific Ocean.

Their conversation was light and easy. "There's the tip of Molokai," he said pointing out his window. She eagerly leaned toward him to get a better look. "In just a few minutes we'll pass close to Maui."

After the easy landing, Derick took her hand in his as they walked briskly to the car rental agencies. His preference was for a convertible and he was given a little red sports car.

As they sped down the highway, their hair blowing in the wind, April was intrigued by the sights. "I expected to see lots of flowers and all I see is rocks," she chuckled as she surveyed the black lava surrounding the area.

"You'll see flowers," he guaranteed, "when you drive into the mountains. I'll draw a map for you. You'll not only see rugged coastlines, but a volcano, sugar cane fields, and lots of flowers. Can you imagine all of that on this little island that is only 93 miles long?"

As they drove with the ocean in view, the water reminded April of blue ink spilled on a blotter. The waves came in like poured sugar. The afternoon sun burned but the wind kept them from feeling its affect. The barren lava stretched on for miles. "This is Kona," Derick said matter-of-factly. The town was small but charming as it spread itself along the ocean. Bright pink bougain-villea bloomed next to the landmark church in the town's center. Hotels with green lawns were strung along the coast.

"There aren't too many beaches that are good for sunbathing," Derick explained. "So you will probably want to spend your time sightseeing."

Derick stopped the car in front of a small real estate office. He took a piece of paper from his briefcase and began drawing a map.

"Have you ever seen a volcano before?" he asked.

"Are you kidding. I've hardly been out of Minnesota, remember?"

"Here, follow this," he said shoving his map with its squiggly lines into her hands. "This will take you a couple of hours. Meet me back here at 5:30." April watched as he confidently walked into the building with its many real estate advertisments.

April studied his map and then steered the sports car onto the highway as she began her trek through the island. The map was precisely drawn and easy to follow. Soon she left the coast route and found herself in the midst of a lush green, tropical forest. "What a change," she marveled.

Over an hour had passed when she saw road signs pointing to the Volcano House and Crater Rim Drive. She decided to pull into the hotel's parking lot.

April visited the gift shop buying several postcards and two pounds of Kona coffee—one for T.J. and one for Uncle David. Maybe I'm trying to ease my guilt for taking the afternoon off, she reasoned.

She wondered if she would have time to watch the film of a recent volcanic eruption. It was being shown in the park museum. Deciding it was now or never, she found a seat in the back of the little theatre. The film kept her spellbound.

Time was getting away as she hurried to her car. I don't want to be the brunt of Derick's wrath by being late, she thought. The winding roads made the driving slow. A slight drizzle forced her to stop and put the top up on the convertible. She passed few cars and noticed no signs of life as she continued descending.

The drizzle turned to a steady rain. Without warning, smoke bellowed from the front of her car. Panic seized her. A red light on the dashboard indicated trouble. She guided the car to the side of the road and buried her head in her arms on the steering wheel.

"What's wrong with this car?" she cried out to no one in particular. She shut off the engine, got out of the car and attempted to open the hood. She didn't know how to open it and realized she wouldn't know what to do if she could. She only succeeded in getting herself wet. She tried to remember if she had passed any gas stations on her drive up. She would be drenched if she tried to walk and she knew she wouldn't make it far in her high heels.

She heard a car approaching. As she looked back, it passed her whizzing down the road. The rain began to let up as dusk set in. She watched several other cars pass. It was only a half hour now until Derick would be expecting her. What would he think when she wasn't there? Would he be furious? Surely his impatience wouldn't let him fly back to Honolulu without her. Fear gripped her as her imagination got carried away. Surely a Good Samaritan would come by soon.

Time crept by as she waited in the car. If everything had gone right, she would be enjoying a romantic dinner with Derick. Would he be worrying about her or just frustrated?

Another forty minutes passed. Then April heard the rumbling of a truck. "Thank you, God," she muttered as she watched the truck slow down and then pull over to the side of the road. The driver came to the window of April's car and asked, "You havin' problems, miss?"

"Yes," she nervously said. "I think it might

be the radiator. Smoke keeps coming out."

He produced a flashlight from his truck and then propped open the hood on the convertible.

"Yep," he said. 'You've got a broken radiator hose. You won't find anything open around here tonight. You better let me give you a lift. Where are you headed?"

"I was supposed to meet a friend in Kona" she anxiously said glancing at the time. "That was hours ago."

"I'm headed that way. I'll take you," the kind man offered.

"Thanks for stopping," April meekly said as the truck barreled down the mountain. "I was beginning to think I was going to spend the night there."

April felt at ease with the driver as they chatted about his wife and four children, his job in the sugar cane fields, and the odds that he happened to be traveling that route later than usual.

After traveling for more than an hour, April's battered spirits brightened as the village lights came into view. As they entered Kona, April directed him to the real estate office where she had left Derick. Her heart sank as she saw no lights on in the tiny office. There's no telling where I will find Derick, she worried. For all I know he might be back in Honolulu.

The driver stopped the truck in front of the real

estate office. April climbed out saying, "Maybe he left a note for me on the door." Seeing none, she dejectedly turned away.

Then a thought struck her. Perhaps there's a number to call in case of emergency. She walked back to the door and her spirits lifted as she spotted the emergency number. She jotted down the digits and looked around for a telephone booth. Confident that the real estate man could offer some clues as to Derick's whereabouts, she dialed the number.

She was elated when she heard a man answer the phone. "This is April Anderson," she began. "I was to meet Derick Donovan at your real estate office at 5:30. Unfortunately, my car broke down and I was terribly delayed. Would you know where I might find him?" her voice was weak.

"Thank goodness, you're all right," came the exuberant response. "Derick has been worried sick about you. He called the police but they wouldn't help search for you until you had been missing 24 hours. He's been calling all the ranger stations. Why, he's even hired a private helicopter to look for you." April was taken aback by Derick's obvious concern for her. "You're a lucky lady. That man really cares about you." April blushed at the thought and decided against explaining their relationship. Maybe beneath Derick's crusty exterior there was a soft core.

"Derick is at his house," the gentleman continued. "Here's his number—872-5731."

"Thanks," April said sheepishly. The real estate man had thought they were romantically involved. April grinned at the idea. Maybe, just maybe he was beginning to show a concrete interest in her, she fantasized. She felt guilty about the anxiety she had caused Derick.

She dialed Derick's number surprised that he had a house here too. It rang busy. She sighed and then tried again.

"Derick," she said, her voice sounding faint. "I'm sorry for the trouble I've caused you. I had car trouble but I finally got a ride to Kona."

"Where are you now?" he demanded, his voice sounded gruff.

"At the real estate office, in a phone booth."

"Stay right there," he boomed. "I'll be there in five minutes."

"All right," she meekly said as she hung up the phone. For someone worried about her, he sure lacked gentleness. The real estate man must have confused his concern for inconvenience.

He startled her as he approached her in the darkness of the night. She was acutely aware of his arm on her shoulder. She collapsed in his arms as he gently held her. When he tightened his grip, she felt safe and secure and perfectly at ease. Tiredness ached in her bones.

He led her to the car without speaking. As he began to drive, she apologized, "I'm really sorry, Derick. The radiator hose broke. There wasn't much traffic on the road and no one would stop." He still didn't say a word until she asked, "Are we going to fly back tonight?"

"No, it's too late. The airport closes at 9 P.M."

"Where are we going then?"

"To my house," was his simple answer.

"Derick, what's wrong?" April pleaded.

"I'll miss a very important business breakfast tomorrow." His tone was flat.

"I'm sorry," April pleaded for forgiveness as if it were her fault. Her words seem futile. "Can't you reschedule it?"

"No," he curtly replied. "The banker leaves for Singapore at 8:30. Tomorrow's meeting would have clinched the deal."

He stopped the car in front of a small house situated on a cliff overlooking the vast expanse of water. Silently they walked into the house. "Derick," April begged for his attention, "you shouldn't have missed that meeting because of me. You could have flown back without me." Her eyes felt hot and congested from unshed tears.

"It's all right," his tone was lifeless. He gathered her in his arms. He kissed her tenderly on the forehead and smoothed back her mangled hair.

She gained her composure, her eyes darted around the house wondering about the sleeping accommodations. Sensing her worry, he put his finger beneath her chin and forced her to look him in the eye.

"Forget all your wild fantasies of seduction your imagination has conjured up," he said. "It's time you went to bed—alone."

April watched as Derick walked away and then returned with a pillow and blanket. "You take the bedroom, and I'll sleep here on the couch."

"Oh, no," she protested. "I'll sleep on the couch. After all, this is your place."

"No," his word was firm and final.

The next morning she dressed in her crumpled clothes. Hearing Derick in the kitchen, she timidly joined him, feeling the pain and anguish she had caused him.

"Well, the princess awakens," he said facetiously. She was wary of his smile. He's probably making fun of my appearance she thought. She had no makeup and her comb would not tame the tangles from her fitful night of sleep.

"Derick, I'm really sorry about last night." She again tried to soothe his angry mood.

"That's all behind us now," he said, handing her a cup of black coffee.

The sea air was crisp in the early morning hour as they drove the sedan rental car to the airport.

April was quiet as she took in her last view of the island of Hawaii. She delighted in hearing the mynah birds chattering under the coco palms.

Derick's plane was ready to go when they arrived at the airport. They quickly boarded. The takeoff was smooth and April glued her eyes to the window as the island disappeared below. Their conversation was stilted during the 40-minute ride back to Honolulu International.

Chapter 13

After a quick shower and change of clothes, April hurried to the gallery. She had a 10:30 appointment with a prospective manager for the gallery. He had a very impressive resume.

As April interviewed Michael Beith for the job, she felt a kinship with the robust, middle-aged man. He had many years of experience in the art business and only recently had moved to Honolulu from New York City due to his wife's health.

"I'd like you to start right away," April told him.

"I'd be delighted to," he replied.

The rest of the day was taken up with details for the benefit. April had brought a portable TV from the Martins' so that she and Tessie could watch T.J. on his interview program. He unveiled two of his works on the talk show and encouraged the viewers to stop by the gallery during his 10-day exhibition.

Tonight was Mona's garden party. April had seen the guest list and was impressed to see that the mayor and his wife were attending as well as many of Hawaii's elite citizens. It promised to be quite a social event.

"I'll pick you up at 6:45," T.J. said, poking his head into April's office. "Don't keep me waiting."

"Not on your life," she retorted. Tired of pushing papers and making last-minute decisions, April was glad when she could leave the gallery. She worried about what to wear, wishing she had time to buy a new outfit. "They'll have to take me as I am," she sighed, "I'm not out to impress anyone, so I'll just blend into the background."

In frustration she searched through her closet. Her clothes were too down-home with no flare of sophistication. She realized there was no way she could compete with the caliber of women who would be at the garden party.

Days earlier she had looked forward to this big evening. Now she found herself almost dreading it. Not only did she not have the proper attire but she realized she wouldn't know many people. T.J. was never at a loss for words and would be busy conversing with everyone he met.

After settling on her hot-pink dress, she heard T.J.'s rental car and hurried down the staircase.

As she opened the door, he gave her his nod of approval. She surveyed her escort and flirted, "My, but you look dapper."

"You don't think I'm overdressed?" he asked in an expression of undeniable pride. He was wearing light beige trousers with a nubby tweed sports jacket. His tan shirt was open at the neck, displaying a fine gold chain. "Honolulu is pretty casual," he worried.

"But you're the guest of honor and you look fabulous," April comforted him.

The directions were easy to follow as they wound their way out of the city limits. Their course took them along the coast into a wealthy residential area.

"This must be the place," T.J. said as he saw the massive Mercedes-Benz traffic jam. A white wooden house was set behind a circular driveway. Large palm trees lined the street. The estate was surrounded by a white wooden fence.

April felt the butterflies in her stomach as they walked to the backyard feeling that she was way out of her league socially.

"Just look," April gasped as she and T.J. entered the expanse of lush green grass lit by torches. Her eyes focused on the tennis court, then the swimming pool, the exquisite rose garden, and the round tables set for dinner. Men and women were milling around sipping cool drinks. April began to feel self-conscious in her simple dress as she saw the women in a riotous array of butterfly colors, subtly and not-so-subtly walking around the garden.

"Throw your shyness to the wind," T.J. urged. "Tonight we're dining with the elite."

April laughed and began to relax when she spotted Mona approaching. The hostess was smiling as she welcomed the guest of honor and his companion.

The colorful tropical flowers brought the backyard to life. Bougainvillea was plentiful and the plumeria trees sprayed the ground with their tiny white flowers. A cascading waterfall spilled into ponds that abounded with plantlife and fish.

Mona was eager to introduce T.J. to her guests. She led the duo to several of her friends who were seated in white wicker furniture.

"I would like you to meet April Anderson, who has been managing the gallery and planning the benefit," Mona gushed. "Of course, you've heard me talk about my good friend T.J., probably the greatest contemporary artist of our time."

April noticed T.J. was flattered by her comments, although he pretended humility. The guests, interested in T.J.'s art, bombarded him with quesitons. April listened and was honored to be among the crowd. When the chattering subsided, she leaned to T.J. and whispered, "Excuse me, I would like to stroll in the rose garden."

"Sure," he replied, giving her a fatherly pat.

She stopped to smell the crimson, pink, and yellow rosebuds before leisurely walking to the pool. She watched from a distance as other arriving guests hugged each friend in warm greeting. A cluster of men were deep in conversation nearby—obviously the athletic type who were talking about their golf scores, she decided.

At the cabana, April picked up a frosty drink with a pineapple wedge propped on the edge of the glass. She gazed intently at the surroundings and then mentally calculated the number of people present. Each table was decorated with pastel green cloths and yellow candles were surrounded by baby orchids.

She joined Mona who was carrying a large silver tray laden with tiny sandwiches and asked, "Is there anything I can do to help?"

"Not a thing, dear," she said setting the tray on the buffet table. "I hope you're enjoying yourself." Mona is the perfect hostess, April thought to herself.

Near the buffet table stood an easel holding a 24"x36" canvas, although it was covered with a heavy white cloth. Did T.J. bring one of his paintings for display, she wondered?

April put it out of her mind when she saw the spread on the buffet table. Fresh fruit was piled high in a watermelon basket. Lead cut crystal bowls were filled with other fruits in monochromatic combinations. Fresh vegetables were dramatically displayed in what looked more like a work of art than something edible. Assorted cheeses and cold cuts were placed near an array of breads. This was just hors d'oevres!

"What a romantic refuge," she said daydreaming of a garden wedding. She shuddered at the thought which left her with a feeling of aloneness.

A Hawaiian musical group began setting up their microphones and sound equipment. Three men were dressed in identical white slacks and colorful orange flowered shirts.

T.J. escorted April to their assigned table. After a quick round of introductions, laughter and chatter filled the balmy night air.

The Hawaiian trio began a musical repertoire that ranged from Hawaiian classsics to mellow love songs.

"This is one of the most exciting nights of my life," April whispered to T.J., beaming from ear to ear.

When she finished eating her salad, almost disbelieving her invitation to such a gathering, she viewed the boundaries of the garden and noticed two late-arriving guests. Her heart lurched as she recognized the tall, lean figure. Derick was accompanying Pat.

Pat, wearing a smart black tunic over black pants, was attracting attention as she slowly made her way into the garden on crutches. Derick, a model of casual chic, was wearing all white.

April did her best to gain her composure. She didn't want anyone at their table to notice that his presence gave her schoolgirl jitters. She tried to find a neutral place to rest her eyes but couldn't help but notice as Derick chivalrously helped Pat into her seat. He propped her crutches nearby and then took the seat next to her. It was obvious to April they knew all the guests at their table, including the mayor.

The waiter set down a plate of lobster thermidor, fresh asparagus, and rice pilaf in front of each guest. April pretended to be hungry although now her stomach felt like a tempest in a teacup. From the corner of her eye, she watched as Derick surveyed the other guests. She felt the color rise in her cheeks as his eyes settled on her. There was something disarming about his smile. She coyly looked away refusing to meet his gaze.

T.J. asked her a question and, flustered, she

had to ask him to repeat it. As she answered, she tenderly touched his arm hoping Derick would notice.

It seemed to April that Pat was the center of attraction at her table as she gestured boldly while she talked. April had never known such a mingling of emotions. One minute she despised the man, but she could never stay angry at him. Is it just a crush, she wondered, or am I falling in love with him? How can I love someone who is only interested in his work, she questioned. Then too, there's no way I could ever compete with Pat's power and position. When Derick has been attentive, he's probably just showing sympathy for this unsophisticated midwestern girl, she ruefully decided.

"You can count on Mona to plan a perfect party," one of the ladies interrupted her thoughts, and the others chimed in their agreement.

April gave her attention to the musical group as they sang "The Hawaiian Wedding Song." She was again aware of Derick's eyes scanning her. She found herself snuggling closer to T.J. so that Derick would have a good show. T.J. didn't mind the attention she was suddenly showering on him. "There's no way I want Derick to ever know my feelings about him," she resolutely told herself.

When the music finished, Mona's husband took the microphone. "Ladies and gentlemen, we have a surprise for you this evening. As you know, we're deeply honored to have the great artist, T.J. Richard, with us tonight. Sunday night we'll all see his work at Gottery Gallery. T.J., come up here and tell us about this surprise.''

April looked at him quizzically. He hadn't told her about any surprise. He patted her shoulder as he stood up and walked to the microphone.

Applause filled the air. "When I learned the proceeds of the benefit would go toward establishing an annual scholarship fund for art students, well, I was overwhelmed when I heard it would be named after me. Therefore, I wanted to do something special for this fund. I've done a special portrait and am donating the proceeds of it entirely to the scholarship fund." There was more applause before he could continue. "Secret bids will be taken for this painting and the highest bidder will walk away with this portrait and the satisfaction of being the first to contribute to the scholarship fund."

Applause roared through the garden amid the smiles of pleasure. "I'd like to ask April Anderson, who has organized my exhibition, to help me unveil this painting," T.J. continued.

April blushed but shyly joined T.J. next to the easel. They each took a corner of the fabric and pulled it back to reveal a pastel painting of a young girl in a striking pose. April regained her breath and a degree of poise as she realized the artist had captured the exact shade of her blue eyes, her sun-kissed blonde hair and the warmth of her smile. It's not exactly me, April realized, as she studied the strong resemblances. Technically the painting was well-done but April was sure she didn't possess that soft, vulnerable look.

T.J. publicly thanked her for her assistance as she slipped back to her seat. "As I mentioned," he continued, "anyone interested in helping the scholarship fund and owning this painting, just write your bid on a piece of paper and give it to our gracious hostess. She'll tally the results."

April was embarrassed to look at the portrait as she watched the other guests crowd forward. She saw Pat alone at her table and timidly approached her.

"I'm glad to see you're out of the hospital" she said lightly.

"Thanks," Pat smiled. "I hear things are coming along fine for the benefit. I'm really looking forward to seeing all of T.J.'s works. He's a marvelous artist."

"It will be quite an event," April replied knowing her voice sounded stiff. "I'll see you Sunday night," and then she began wandering aimlessly through the garden.

"April," Derick's voice deepened as he said her name. She turned around and met his gaze.

"I didn't realize you were a model, too," he said gently as the significance of his words sank in April's mind. "I imagine you had to spend a lot of hours with the artist. Was it all work?" he probed.

With as much dignity as she could muster, April responded, "If you're hinting that I might be romantically interested in T.J., the answer is 'No.' " She noticed the muscles in his face relax. Had she aroused his jealousy?

Before walking away, he gently stroked her arm sending shivers up her back. "You're doing a magnificent job," he complimented her. His touch was magnetic.

April watched him leave. He graciously helped Pat with her crutches and they slowly walked to the painting for a closer look.

The guests were starting to leave, even though it was not late. April was content to stand in the distance. She watched Mona, seated at a table, sorting through the bids. Suddenly Mona animately began talking with Pat and Derick. Derick tenderly kissed the hostess on the cheek and then carefully took the painting from the easel.

"Oh, no," April gasped. "Pat's bought the painting," as she watched the two exit from the garden. "She thinks it's a good investment. It's too great to be stored in a vault while she waits for the value to go up," she lamented.

T.J. interrupted her worries as he asked if she were ready to leave.

"Sure," she smiled weakly. "Let's say good night to Mona."

Her words were sincere but shallow as she tried to thank her hostess. Spontaneously she hugged Mona, a woman who had come to mean a great deal to her.

As soon as she and T.J. were out of earshot from the other guests, she squealed at him. "You didn't tell me about the painting!"

"Don't you like surprises?" he teased.

She nodded and then cautiously remarked, "People saw a resemblance of me in the painting."

"You were my inspiration," he said grinning.

Flattered she went on, "That was a lovely thing to do, T.J. I mean, donating the funds to the scholarship program. By the way, do you know how much money the painting brought?"

"Would you believe," he said with pride in his voice, "$25,000? That tops my previous sales."

April gulped. "Twenty-five-thousand dollars! And I thought Pat only looked for bargains for investment purposes."

"Pat?" T.J. gave her a strange look. "She didn't buy it. Derick did,"

Chapter 14

April was stunned as she rode in silence, causing T.J. to finally ask, "Are you feeling okay?"

"Oh, I'm fine," she forced herself to answer brightly. "Just tired," she fibbed and faked a yawn.

Her mind was searching for answers. Why did Derick buy the portrait? Was it to ridicule her or was he sincerely interested in helping an art student? He had seen the likeness of her in the portrait. Maybe he sees me as one of his blasted investments. She seethed as the thought crossed her mind. Maybe he has a trophy room in one of his houses where he hangs portraits of girls he has romanced. An expression of rage and frustration overtook her.

She was glad when she could escape from T.J.'s watchful eyes. "Don't bother to walk me to the door," she said softly as she slipped out of the car. Then she turned to wave good night.

She paced through the house turning on all the lights. A craziness ran through her body as she tried to find answers. She would be glad when she could be home in Minneapolis and she and Derick could resume their separate lives.

The night air had turned cool as she walked into the backyard. She stretched out on a chaise lounge by the pool. The stars twinkled overhead and the moon cast an eerie shadow across the backyard as she tried to piece together the puzzle.

She saw the picture emerge. She cared for Derick more than she wanted to admit. Seeing him with Pat tonight stung. She shivered. A rush of misery, an overwhelming sense of loss welled up inside her, catching her by surprise. He had told her from the start he didn't have time for marriage and family. Pat probably understood that and was willing to meet him on his terms.

Chagrined that she had been unable to control her heart's desire, she slowly walked indoors and climbed the stairs to her bedroom.

The next morning the jangle of the alarm clock

startled her from her dream. What a silly dream, she moaned, and then realized her subconscious thoughts had been on Derick.

She dressed casually and after a hurried breakfast, drove to the gallery. She needed to spend time with Michael, showing him the ropes. He's got far more years in the business than I have, she convinced herself, knowing the gallery would be in good hands.

Tessie and Michael greeted her as she arrived.

"It was a great party last night, wasn't it?" Michael exclaimed enthusiastically.

"I've never been to anything quite like it," April sincerely said.

"Has Mr. Donovan bought paintings from Gottery Gallery before?' Michael quizzed her.

"Not to my knowledge," April replied, wondering if he suspected her true feelings for Derick. "In fact, I wasn't aware that he was even interested in art." Her tone was almost sarcastic as she remembered the bare walls of his condo.

"Well, he's got a masterpiece now," Michael said. "And his $25,000 will be an added bonus to the T.J. Scholarship Fund."

April was glad when the conversation ended. There was mounds of paperwork she needed to discuss with Michael. The day passed quickly with a myriad of details for Sunday's benefit. There were dozens of calls of people wanting to make last-minute reservations. April was astonished to find that more than 250 people had responded to the invitations.

"I hope they don't all come at once," she said to Michael as she surveyed the size of the gallery.

When April heard Derick's car leave late that night, she realized there was no chance of confronting him as to his purpose in buying the painting. It still bewildered her.

Saturday afternoon, April and Michael were arranging T.J.'s exhibit when they turned to see Derick's bronzed face in the doorway.

"Just stopped by to see how things are coming along for tomorrow night," he inquired with extreme politeness.

April was glad when Michael took over the conversation. "That was quite a feat buying T.J.'s painting at the garden party, Mr. Donovan. You've made some unknowing art students very happy. Would you like to have an advance look at T.J.'s display?" Michael asked, convincing April she had hired a good salesman.

"No, no, I'll wait until tomorrow like everyone else," he shrugged his shoulders.

April wished she could have talked with Derick alone. Then it dawned on her. He had said tomorrow. That meant he would be here with Pat. Her heart was heavy as she thought about it. Determined not to get sidetracked dreaming of Derick, she walked around the gallery to see if everything was in order for tomorrow night.

T.J. unexpectedly stopped by and announced he was taking everyone to dinner. April tried to join in the frivolities as they dined at one of Honolulu's finest restaurants. The scenery from the skytop room was breathtaking and the food was superbly prepared, but April's heart was in turmoil. This city was one of the most beautiful she had ever seen and the people here had made her trip unforgettable. When she thought of the people, she naturally reflected on Derick. He was one of Honolulu's most eligible bachelors but was completely absorbed in his work, and unfortunately that included his partner Pat.

April was relieved when T.J. suggested leaving, anticipating the duties of tomorrow's big event.

After Sunday's worship service, she thanked Pastor Andrews for his thought-provoking sermons. "I'll be leaving Honolulu tomorrow," she explained.

Too excited to eat lunch, April slipped into her jeans and the pink T-shirt Stanley had bought her. I wonder what ever happened to good ole Stanley, she thought. Just like a man, she realized—he said he would call and never did.

Chapter 15

*A*pril's heart fluttered as she drove to the gallery even though she knew everything was organized—Mona had seen to that.

As she unlocked the gallery and wondered what to do first, the caterers arrived and began setting up their tables. They brought in boxes of silver trays, coffee urns, white china plates and cups. From their refrigerated truck they brought in huge trays of sumptuous-looking hors d'oeuvres covered with plastic wrap. It all looked so tempting.

Mona soon arrived with her husband, giving him instructions to put the silver mylar balloons outside, marking the entrance. The valet attendants arrived for their duties. Meg and Stephanie arrived the same time as the florist. April was astonished at the transformation of the gallery in just a few minutes. I believe these ladies have done this before, she raved.

By 4:30 all the work was done. The women rushed off to change clothes with the promise of returning soon. T.J. arrived and it was obvious he was excited and nervous. He had been the center of attention at art exhibits before, but nothing as extravagant as this.

"You'd better get dressed," he nervously whispered to April. "I'll take over now."

Twenty minutes of primping and April felt revitalized as she emerged from the ladies room wearing her new silk blouse with the slinky pants and high heels. Her gold earrings dangled as she moved her head.

She felt euphoric as she took her place at the door welcoming each guest. She pointed them in the direction of the buffet table and encouraged them to browse through the gallery.

Verbal bouquets abounded as people admired the paintings and the gallery. This all bolstered April's shaky ego until she became positively giddy with excitement.

T.J. caught her eye and gave her the "thumbs up" signal. She was thrilled that he was pleased with the exhibition. She had fought the obstacles and emerged triumphantly. Thinking back to her first day at the gallery, she remembered feeling like giving up. Perhaps if it hadn't been for Derick's attitude, which challenged her stubborn spirit, she might have chucked it all. Perhaps he did deserve a word of thanks.

Her heart skipped a beat when she saw Derick arrive with Pat. He looked so handsome and suave. Was he becoming interested in art or was he coming just to please Pat? April managed a feeble smile. The feeling of seeing the two of them together was neither good nor unpleasant, just peculiar.

"You looked radiant," Derick lauded her.

She blushed and thanked him. With a gesture of her hand, she indicated where the line formed for the buffet.

She caught the wink in his eye as he left with Pat. It infuriated her. *He's with another woman but he thinks he can flirt with me.* She bristled at the thought.

It was nearly seven o'clock. April's feet were killing her. She found an empty chair in the corner. When she thought no one was looking, she kicked off her shoes and began rubbing her tired feet.

"Ladies and gentlemen," T.J. shouted above the background noise, attempting to get everyone's attention.

"What's he doing?" April frowned. "We didn't plan on any speeches."

As soon as the gallery quieted down, he continued, "First of all, I want to say how delighted I am that you have all come today. This is one of the most exciting moments of my life. I owe it all to a young girl who, not only gave this gallery new lifeblood, but spearheaded this benefit. I want to publicly thank April Anderson. I think she should come up here and say a few words." The applause was deafening. April scrambled to put her shoes back on.

Her heart thumped. The color drained from her face and her mind seemed to freeze. What was she supposed to say? How could T.J. dare do this to her? Public speaking wasn't one of her talents. She felt the stares as she blindly forced herself to walk forward.

T.J. kissed her on the cheek and firmly gripped her hand as she joined him. The people melted into a vast sea of faces as she began to speak. "I really can't take the credit for tonight," she began. "It's Mona who deserves the credit. She along with Meg, Stephanie, and, and..." she almost stumbled over the next name, "Pat put this benefit together."

She caught sight of Derick as she spoke. His big brown eyes were riveted on her and he had a beguiling smile that captivated her heart.

She took a deep breath and continued, "I've enjoyed my stay in Honolulu but I will be leaving tomorrow so it's Michael Beith you should be getting acquainted with. He's our gallery's new manager." She thought she saw surprise in Derick's eyes but she wasn't sure. "Thanks for coming tonight." She smiled at T.J. and stepped away. The applause rang out as April felt her heart still pounding fiercely. She wasn't even sure what she had said. She only knew she had given a speech and her voice had not quivered. She soon lost herself in the mingling crowd.

As the people started to leave, April felt an immense gratification for the job she had done. "Thank You, dear Jesus," she silently prayed.

From a distance, she caught sight of Derick and Pat exiting. It hurt her to think he hadn't even bothered to say good bye. That's the last I'll ever see of him, she thought, and then realized maybe words left unsaid were better.

She was feeling a great deal of pride in the success of the evening as she watched Michael total the sales. T.J. was still chatting with a few remaining guests while the caterers cleaned up. She felt a light touch on her shoulder and whirled around to encounter Derick's eyes.

"I thought you had left," she managed to stammer.

"I did," he said with a serious look on his face.

"But I came back to talk with you. Do you mind if I take you home?"

"That would be fine," she said, dumbfounded. Her emotions became clouded. What could he possibly want to say to me, she questioned herself.

Disguising her nervousness, she waved good-bye to T.J. and Michael. Derick gently took her elbow and escorted her to his car.

"I'll have to admit," he said as they drove off, "I didn't think you could pull it off when I first met you. But you're quite a lady."

April, unsure whether that was a compliment or a put-down, was quiet as he continued. "You really surprised me, April. You seemed so inexperienced."

She fidgeted at his insinuation and then relaxed as she confessed to him, "I probably owe a lot to you. I think my stubbornness was challenged when I realized you didn't think I could manage the gallery." Her eyes were demurely cast down as she went on. "That's probably what pushed me to succeed. At times I was ready to give up and go back home but I wasn't about to let you think I failed. I remember you told me, 'There are no failures unless they stop you.'"

He looked straight ahead at the road. "One thing has got me baffled. I saw Pat hurt you with words, bitter words. But you never struck back. You even cancelled a date to visit her in the hospital. What made you do that?'' His voice was low but sincere as he asked the question.

April chose her words carefully before she answered. "I'm no match for Pat, that's for sure. It's human nature to want to strike back and I'll admit I wanted to. But I was taught to "do good to those who hate you and pray for those who spitefully use you.'' She laughed, reminded of his jabs as he quoted and misquoted the Bible. "You probably heard that one in Sunday school too.''

He smiled and nodded in agreement. "I've heard it but I've never known anyone to put it into practice.''

"The best way I learned forgiveness is to remind myself of my own faults and weaknesses. I realized if I didn't forgive Pat, that I was doing an even greater disservice to myself.''

She sensed Derick's openness to hear more and continued, "I remember reading once that love is the strongest force in the world and when it is blocked that can only mean pain. There are two things we can do when that happens—either we kill the love so that it stops hurting or we can ask God to open up another route for that love to travel. I tried to block loving Pat and then I realized a part of me was dying. So there was no other way but to ask God to give me a love for her.''

"Love is hard for me to comprehend," Derick

said as he drove from the city lights to the dark residential area. "It's easy to hate but I think love has to be learned. Unfortunately, I haven't learned it. Love has eluded me. That's probably why I have buried myself in my work."

"Perhaps it's easier for those of us who have learned love at an early age. But it's never too late to love." Her heart leaped with joy as she continued, "Because love is not a tangible object, it is hard to define. It's not a feeling that comes from physical stimulation and then fades away.

"The Apostle Paul had some neat things to say about love in 1 Corinthians 13. What he says, in effect, is that he would be worth nothing if he didn't have love. He said even if he gave everything he owned to the poor and consistently preached the gospel, if he didn't love others it would be of no value."

Derick listened as April seized the opportunity to talk about love. "Love doesn't hold grudges."

"I saw that kind of love when you forgave Pat," he said. He pulled into the Martins' driveway and shut off the engine but made no attempt to get out of the car.

"Love is always kind and patient. That's really hard sometimes. Another thing, love is never jealous. That's something I'm still working on," she confessed and then wondered from Derick's look if she had given away her secret feelings for him. She bit her lower lip and continued. "If you truly love someone, you'll be loyal no matter what the cost. You will always believe in him and always expect the best of him. I just want to say, Derick, I wish you the best in everything. I'll be praying that you find the meaning of love. Just remember, those who never love go through life empty handed. I didn't mean to preach," she laughed. "End of sermon."

Seeing his troubled look, she reached over and gently touched his arm. He squeezed her hand. She whispered, "Good-bye, Derick," and gracefully slipped out of the car.

Chapter 16

April's body ached with tiredness but she felt exhilarated as she walked into the house. For once Derick hadn't become angry or turned moody. But best of all, he had listened intently as she shared her Christian values.

Thoughts of Derick controlled her mind as she crawled into bed. Their parting words had been like the melody of a soulful flute instead of their usual discordant music. It's been a fabulous experience, she reflected before drifting off to sleep.

She awoke the next morning as the sun crept into her room. Reveling in the newspaper article describing last night's event, she lingered on the patio and drank her coffee slowly, not really wanting to leave. She felt an odd sense of displacement as she dressed for her last visit to Gottery Gallery.

For the last time, she steered the BMW into the underground parking structure and automatically looked for Derick's car. It wasn't in its usual place. She had said good-bye last night and would savor that precious memory for a long time.

A rising chorus of voices greeted her upon entering the gallery.

"April!" T.J. joyously proclaimed as he picked her up and whirled her around the room. "Do you realize that nearly half of my paintings sold last night. How can I begin to thank you?" he burst with enthusiasm.

April, exuberant, laughed and said, "I have had all the thanks I need," not explaining the self-confidence she had gained through the experience.

"Do you realize we've netted nearly $35,000 for the scholarship fund? The women's committee said they want me back next year. Of course," he flirted, "I only promised to come if you were here."

"I'd like that," she beamed at the idea.

Turning to Michael, she asked, "Do you have any questions before I leave this tropical paradise?"

"Everything's under control," he assured her.

"If I do have any problems, I know where to reach you. We'll see you next year when you return for T.J.'s second annual benefit."

"Well, I can see when I'm no longer needed," she pretended to feel slighted. "Guess I better go home and pack."

"Can we take you to the airport?" T.J. offered.

"No, that's okay," she said. "I'll just call a taxi."

"Thanks, Tessie," she said to the Oriental girl giving her a tight squeeze. "You've been a big help. Thanks, too, for your friendship."

She shook hands with Michael and then turned to T.J. "None of that for me," he teased as he hugged her tightly and gave her a fatherly kiss.

April left the gallery with mixed emotions. She had come to love the islands and its people. She walked to her car and secretly longed for one last glimpse of Derick. His car was still missing in the garage.

She savored remembrances of Honolulu—the huge palm trees with their fronds blowing gently in the breeze, the blue skies and puffy white clouds, the balmy temperature and the fine white sand of Waikiki Beach.

At the Martins', she finished her packing and looked up the telephone number of a taxi. Hearing a car in the driveway, she walked to the window to peer out. A long white limousine parked near the front door. Perhaps the Martins had arrived earlier than planned.

Then her heart throbbed with pleasure as she saw Derick. In his arms he carried a huge purple and white orchid lei.

She rushed to the door before he could knock. As he lovingly put the lei around her neck, he bent to kiss her gently on the lips.

She was speechless as he turned to the chauffeur and said, "Get her bags, please."

"What?" she blurted.

"I'm taking you to the airport." He was adamant as he ignored the astonished look on her face.

The driver put her bags into the trunk as Derick escorted her into the roomy backseat. She gasped. "I've never seen anything like this," she exclaimed as she slid across the black leather upholstery. Then she noticed the portable color TV set, the telephone, and the silver ice bucket holding a bottle of sparkling cider.

As he slid into the seat beside her, she noticed the weary look in his eyes. Was it tiredness or sadness, she wondered.

He felt a need to explain. "I didn't get much sleep last night."

"I'm sorry," she felt compassion for him.

"No, don't be," he said firmly. "Last night after I left you I began to do a lot of soul-searching. I went home and shook the dust off my Bible. I started reading. I wasn't sure where to begin but I remembered John 3:16 from my Sunday school days. For the first time in my life those words had meaning. I wanted to find out more about unconditional love. I wanted to have love like yours. I realized I couldn't imitate yours but wanted to discover the real thing for myself. I realized love is an effect so I studied more and found the cause. As I read 1 John, the words became so plain to me 'We love because He first loved us.' At that moment I surrendered my soul to that kind of love.''

"Oh, Derick, that's wonderful," April cried out as the limo eased its way through the crowded Honolulu streets.

"I saw something different about you when I first met you," Derick went on. "But every time I sensed myself starting to care about you, I fought it. Your sparkle, enthusiasm, and your love for people intrigued me, but I rebelled in accepting that love. I hope you'll forgive me."

"Of course, Derick," April replied, hardly believing her ears.

"There's one more thing," Derick said, deliberately choosing his words. "I've got a lot to learn about love and I, um, I was...wondering if you'd be willing to help me?"

April wasn't sure what he meant and she had

never seen him at a loss for words. He was always so confident and self-assured.

He took some papers from his briefcase. "Would you come back to Honolulu?" he asked handing her an airline ticket.

Stunned she could only stare at him. "Sure," she managed to utter.

"If you'll notice," he softly said. "It's a one-way ticket." She sat motionless, scarcely breathing, fingering the orchids around her neck.

Then to lighten the mood, he said, "It's not always easy being single. When I come home late from the office, no one cares that I missed dinner." April grinned at the thought. "There's no one but me to blame if there's a dent in the Porsche. And like I've always said..." he spoke with a gleam in his eye, "the key to success is diversification!" April smiled at their private joke.

"What I'm trying to say," he said as he tenderly caressed her hand, "is will you promise me you'll love me forever?"

As the significance of his words sunk in, he took out a tiny velvet box. April's mouth widened in amazement as she saw the glitter of the huge sparkling diamond ring.

"It's beautiful, Derick," she gasped as he slipped it on her finger. "But what about Pat?"

"What about Pat?" he was puzzled by her question.

"Well," April began and didn't know exactly how to ask. "She obviously cares a great deal about you...."

"We have a great business arrangement. But that's all," Derick assured her.

Derick gathered her in his arms and she could only surrender.

"I've never said this to anyone before," Derick admitted. "I love you."

"I love you, too, Derick, and promise it's forever."

"Then you'll marry me?"

Gazing lovingly at him she whispered, "I will," and his strong arms held her tightly as he claimed her lips with a tender kiss.